Hook a Fish,
Catch a
Mountain

ALSO BY JEAN CRAIGHEAD GEORGE

Hook a Fish, Catch a Mountain

Jean Craighead George

E. P. DUTTON & CO., INC.   NEW YORK

LIBRARY OF CONGRESS CATALOGING IN PUBLICATION DATA

George, Jean Craighead   Hook a fish, catch a mountain

SUMMARY: After catching a cutthroat, a vanishing species
of fish in the Snake River, Spinner Shafter and her cousin
Alligator do some ecological detecting to determine where
the fish came from and how he had survived.

[1. Cutthroat trout—Fiction.   2. Ecology—Fiction.
3. Fishing—Fiction]   I. Title.
PZ7.G2933Hq   [Fic]   74–23884   ISBN 0–525–32155–1

Published simultaneously in Canada by Clarke,
Irwin & Company Limited, Toronto and Vancouver

Designed by Meri Shardin
Printed in the U.S.A.   First Edition
10   9   8   7   6   5   4   3   2   1

To Cousin Bill Craighead,
the complete fisherman,
and to the trout of Ditch Creek.

CONTENTS

Hook a Fish, Catch a Mountain

FISH

A skinny girl in mountain boots and bulky clothes stood on the bank of the river. She looked like a glass figurine wrapped for shipment. In one hand she held a fishing rod. With the other she pushed the long black hair from her face. It swept below her waist, a gleaming, well-groomed pyramid of lights.

Suddenly the fishing rod bowed like a question mark and the girl braced as a fish took her line. The stones of the gravel bar rolled under her feet and she was pulled into the icy Snake River. The water seeped through the eyelets of her mountain boots. She glanced around desperately. The entire valley of Jackson Hole, Wyoming—its sky and saw-blade mountains, its people and wild things—were conspiring against her. She, Spinner Shafter, age thirteen, a dancer in the Roundelay Dance Company, was about to be drowned by a fish.

"Get in here!" she screamed to the creature pulling her. She dug in her heels, gained a better footing, and yanked.

"Get in here this minute so I never have to fish again . . . ever. . . ." The reel spun like a windmill in a hurricane and the line darted into the sparkling water where Ditch Creek meets the thunderous Snake. Then it moved upstream. Spinner watched with amazement. She could not even stand in the water that roared down from the Yellowstone plateau like a freight train. Yet the fish on the end of her line was pulling hook, line reel, rod, and herself up the roaring flume.

Awed by the strength of the fish, she let him run out the line. Not until the reel screamed to a stop did she remember that she should be reeling in. With great effort she pulled on the line with her free hand.

"You're heavy," she said as she took a wider stance, leaned backward, and gained a meter of line. She reeled in the slack. The stones avalanched under her feet again and delivered her calf-deep into the river. In a moment she would be up to her knees and awash on the curls and tongues of the demonic Snake. Desperately she glanced around for help. Her eyes focused on the mountains. They were no longer the alabaster spires she had admired during the day, but a hostile black wall of ice and granite. The sun, now behind the range, was sending rods of metallic light down the dark canyon. Terror seized her.

"Daddy!" she screamed. "Daddy. Help me!" She was shivering, and her arms, which performed so strongly in cartwheels and handstands, trembled. The fish surged away. Grudgingly she was forced to give back the line she had gained so the fish would not break it. Spinner threw herself backward on the gravel bar and reeled in.

She really wished she could be an excellent fisher for her father's sake. She knew he would like it. Years ago he had nicknamed her Spinner after a fish lure. And when he gave her a fly rod the night she executed a delicate dance solo, it was clear that he wanted a fisher, not a dancer.

"Well, FISH," she said out loud. "He hasn't got one. He hasn't got a fisher to brag about." She paused, then whispered to the river, "A dancer is splendid, dedicated to beauty and movement; it is the most exalted of the arts. A dancer does *not* have to fish!"

She clutched the rod to keep the fish from pulling her

into the river. The line trembled. She pulled. It trembled again. The fish was speaking to her.

"I hear you, FISH," she whispered. "You're fighting for your life out there in that terrible water." Spinner tugged. "I said, 'Hello,'" she called aloud. The fish tugged back. "Is that 'hello' or are you frightened? I am. I've never caught a fish before." The fish tugged twice. "What are you saying? You're asking me to let you go? I will, I will, if you'll come in here and let me show you to my father."

The line went limp.

"What does that mean?" she whispered. "I forget what to do when the line goes limp. Pull in? Yes, yes, Daddy said, 'Keep the line taut.'"

Spinner dropped the rod and grabbed the line. She yanked it in hand over hand, pulling faster and faster to keep the tension on the charging fish. He swirled, not four meters away. The water broke into a shower of twilit bubbles, the line zagged, zigged—and went limp.

"I've lost him!—the big fish I was supposed to catch to beat the family record." She sat down and drooped her head.

Spinner recalled her father saying for the hundredth time, as they were fastening their seat belts on the plane in New York: "We'll get a bigger trout than Uncle

Auggie's record of July 17, 1963." He leaned back and folded his hands on his generous stomach. His thin hair capped his smiling face like an asterisk.

"It's time," the big man said, "to win the family fishing medal back. Your granddad took it from me; my brother Augustus took it from him; and now it's your turn again." He laughed, but somehow Spinner knew it was not funny. Her father wanted that medal back.

The plane took off like a gray swan and Spinner watched New York City shrink, then vanish under the clouds. Gone also were the streets, buildings, apartments, and her mother. She waved weakly to all.

"This summer there'll be three generations of fishermen," her father went on. "Your granddad will be in from California, and there'll be Auggie and me and you kids." He sighed. "We'll give 'em some real competition, you and me, Spinner."

Spinner had wriggled nervously, looked down at her toes, and pointed them. She wondered where she would practice dancing in the little cabin in the West. She was about to ask, but her father launched into a description of the fly he would tie. He would copy a creature of the stream so perfectly it would fool the big fish that dwelled in the deep hole across from the old ferry boat. The fish would snatch it and be caught.

Now, as she sat on the gravel bar, she could see that

ferry. It had been pulled up on land by the National Park Service for a museum. She knew every board in the hull. She had memorized them during the three days her father had given her fishing lessons. The first two days she had done poorly looping the line and tangling it as she cast. Finally, on the third day, her father had shortened her line and she had rolled a fly neatly into the center of the river. "You've got it in your blood," he had shouted. "The third generation of great fishermen! You'll beat all the kids."

"Beat all the kids." She recalled those words as she looked at the hopeless mess of nylon line at her feet. "Me from the city," she mused, "competing with two boys who fish from dawn to dusk. Some chance I've got against Paul, who's been fishing since he was born nineteen years ago."

". . . or for that matter," she said out loud to the fish, "some chance I've got against the kid my age, that boy, Al. Al for Alligator." She chuckled at her nickname for him. She called him Alligator because he grinned and grunted and never said more than "umph" or "hmmm."

"Umph," she mimicked. Alligator was probably landing a trophy right now. He knew all the good holes and where the big fish went at twilight. He had dashed past her this evening like a prong-horned antelope to get that spot where the Snake dug a dark den beneath a fallen cottonwood tree. What could she do against a boy like that or against Paul, who had claimed the riverbank across from the old ferry, where the "big one" lay? By the time she had tied on her fly there was no place to fish but the pool off the bar at Ditch Creek. Her father had turned it over to her after catching a snag.

She had cast her line listlessly. The pool was the first river stop at the end of the fishermen's path, and it was, according to her fishing relatives, "all fished out."

Spinner kicked her tangled line and felt almost relieved that the fish was gone—almost. She had seen him and he had been as big as a whale. She only hoped no one had seen her lose him.

Cautiously she peered through the golden twilight. A tanager sang his last song of the day from the tip of a willow branch. The wind rippled the tall green grass of the bank. Nobody had seen. She blew a long breath and looked at her fingers; they were cricked into the shape of the rod handle. She forced them open, the well-trained hands that had been the envy of her dance companions only a week ago. Now they were claws.

Almost in tears, she tried to unsnarl her line, gave up and hauled the mess up on the bank. Suddenly the line tightened and cut a Z in the rough water. Spinner grabbed it with both hands and was yanked to her feet like a water skier. Down to the river's edge she was pulled again.

For an instant the sun struck the water and the bottom of the pool gleamed like a spindle of silver. Then the water rippled and the gleam was gone. "Wild craziness," she thought, "but for in instant I saw tapestry in the river."

Spinner turned, put the line over her shoulder, and slavelike, hauled it up the bar. At the top she threw herself forward and jumped into the quieter waters of Ditch Creek. She struggled to a large log that was jammed against the bank, looped her line around a snag, pulled, and wrapped it once more. When the line was secure she leaned out and hitched in another loop. This, too, she wrapped on the snag.

"You've got a log." It was her father's voice. "Broke my line on it."

"A log?" she cried. "I've got a trout! Help me!" He did not stir.

"By golly," he said. "You do have a fish. Pick up your rod. You can land him." He glanced around nervously. Spinner realized he was embarrassed. "You've got a nice whitefish there, now land him correctly."

"I've got a trout! A cutthroat trout. I saw his big dorsal fin . . . like in the book."

"There're *no* cutthroats in this part of the Snake. Haven't been for years."

Spinner felt the strength seep out of her body. She stumbled and tried to haul in more line. She had to believe her father. Well, whatever the fish was she would land it right in front of him and promptly announce she would never fish again.

"Geez! She's got a beaut!" Alligator was on the other side of Ditch Creek. He had spoken a complete sentence. Spinner looked at him. His T-shirt flapped against his ribby chest and his bronze hair curved over his forehead like a metal helmet. His pale eyes twinkled like pinheads on either side of his large nose. She wished the grass would grow five meters tall and hide him forever.

"Spinner!" her father shouted. "Get your rod. Land this thing right."

"Let her alone." Her grandfather was speaking. He was here too. Spinner stared at the river, feeling the eyes of the three generations of fishermen upon her. They were watching her fish like a cavewoman. She could sense their contempt. But what could she do? She had to keep tension on the fishline and she had to keep out of the terrible river. The fish dashed toward the wild water again, and she lunged, wrapped the line around her hand three times, and tugged.

"Whitefish?" her grandfather asked.

"Yeah," said her father.

"It's a cutthroat!" she shrieked.

The fish turned and came toward her. She reefed in, ran up the bar, and threw herself down on her stomach. She rolled several times and took up the line with her body.

"For geez sake, Spinner!" her father shouted. "Get up and fish." He laughed nervously. "She can do better than that, she really can."

"Wow!" Uncle Augustus had arrived. He whistled and jumped to the gravel bar. His face was serious but kind.

"Nice going, Spinner," he said, and for the first time she liked Uncle Augustus. She sat up. Alligator leaped to her side, crouched silently, and studied the end of her line.

"It's a whopper!" he said.

"It sure is." Paul had arrived. A mountaineering teacher in the Tetons, Paul was an awesome and unreal person to Spinner. He had come down from his work for the evening to fish with the three generations. Paul seemed aware of her for the first time.

"Those whitefish really put on a show," her father said. "And so does Spinner. Very dramatic kid."

Alligator grunted in her ear, "Help?"

"No!" she snapped. "I'll mess this up my own way." She pulled, the line cut into her hand, but she felt no pain; her fingers were too cold to be sensitive.

As the men watched she inched the fish toward shore. The water boiled like a geyser basin, and the light from the setting sun colored the bubbles red and purple. Suddenly the surface exploded like a flame and a huge head rose into view. Uncle Augustus gasped. Alligator whistled. Her father made no sound. The fish lunged toward the channel, turned, and shot back to the gravel bar. His huge dorsal fin emerged above water.

"Cutthroat!" Alligator exclaimed.

"Cutthroat?" It was Paul. "Can't be."

"Oh, FISH," Spinner whispered. "You *are* a cutthroat. I know you are. Come in out of the water so Daddy will be proud of me. He'll throw you back. I promise, I promise. He always throws fish back."

Spinner wriggled up the bar hauling on the line with all her strength. Alligator reached out to help. She shook her head furiously and clutched the line at the water's surface. She yanked it in. The fish splashed near her boot, then rolled to his side, and lay still. He was almost as tired as she, but not quite; with a powerful twist he flipped out of water. He fell into the pool and disappeared from sight.

"No!" Spinner stood up and hurled herself backward. The fish came with her, out of the water, up the stones, to the very top of the bar. He flopped, tore the hook from his mouth, and was free. With a twist he catapulted himself into the air and landed inches from the river. One more flop and he would be gone. Spinner threw herself upon him. The great trout was caught.

"Bravo!" her father cheered.

"Monster," yelled Alligator.

Her father's hand shot past her face. He drove his fingers into the gills of the fish and held him captive. Spinner rolled to her back exhausted and looked up as her father slowly lifted the great fish up against the sky. The speckles on his back and side glowed so brightly he seemed to be lit from within. His belly glowed orange and the red marks under his jaw that gave him the name "cutthroat" gleamed like rubies. His tail was an enormous fan, his body a torpedo. No one spoke for a long moment.

"I think she's got the record." Grandfather finally said. He chuckled.

"I don't know," Uncle Augustus chided. "Doesn't look so big to me." FISH twisted in her father's hand

and his gills opened, then slowly closed. His back shone blue. She had caught a fish, a magnificent fish. She laughed joyously. FISH's round eye bulged and she realized the air was suffocating him.

"Let him go!" Spinner screamed. "Daddy, let him go before he dies!"

"Oh, no. Not this fellow. He's a record. He's the one I've been waiting for!"

"But you said so. You said you throw fish back."

"Not the king of 'em all. Not the family record."

She was stunned. "Daddy, please!"

"Not on your life. We mount this one and hang him over the fireplace." He held the fish higher. "Beat you, Auggie, beat you."

"Spinner beat me," Uncle Augustus said, "not you."

Slowly Spinner got to her feet. Her father clapped her on the back as if she were some boxing champion.

"Nice going, kid," he whooped. "Nice going." He leaped to the bank, held FISH high, then strode up the trail toward the cabin.

"Hmmm," Alligator said as he meekly handed Spinner her rod. "Nifty fish." She began reeling in. A knot caught in the first grommet, snarled, and hung from her rod like last summer's bird nest. Spinner reached into her fishing vest, took out a small pair of embroidery scissors, and cut the line. "I should have done that an hour ago," she said, thrust the rod over her shoulder, and pushed past Alligator to the trail. With a twist of her head she flipped her hair at everyone.

Suddenly she was cold. The temperature had dropped with the setting of the sun, and every muscle in her body was chilled. Spinner could not stop shaking.

"Are you okay?" Grandfather called after her. She did not answer for fear of bursting into tears.

"You did beat Augustus, you know." The old man's gray eyes sparkled under his floppy hat. "That fish is at least two kilograms, maybe three. He's amazing . . . a cutthroat. The last of a native species that once filled these western rivers. Trash fish are now competing with the cutthroats for food. They are pushing them close to extinction." The grand old man grinned, his teeth gleaming like ancient ivory. "And to think you caught one, Spinner. That's nice—a vanishing species." He shook his head, stepped lightly over a log in the path, and followed his sons and grandsons.

Spinner wondered where he had come from, the fish that was one of the last of his kind on earth. Suddenly up ahead in the dark her father trumpeted like a bull elephant. "Wow, we've won! We've won!"

"Not until it's weighed and measured," Paul shouted.

Grandfather whistled and in the darkness Spinner

felt tears of anger flow down her cheeks. She had been deceived; her father had kept a prize trout.

At the far side of the cottonwood grove the bank climbed steeply for five meters to the top of the second bench of the river. It was here the ancient Snake flowed ten thousand years ago. Halfway up, Spinner, exhausted by the fish, dropped to her hands and knees and crawled to the top. The lights of Uncle Augustus' house blinked warmly in the distance.

Aunt Becky would be putting on a pot of coffee. The planet Venus was sitting on the top of Buck Mountain. It marked the time the fishermen came home from the river. Spinner wiped her tears and ran toward Aunt Becky.

THE CARTWHEEL

The next morning Spinner awoke in the little log-walled room off the kitchen. Cold air wafted in through the open window. She smelled its wild freshness and listened to the stir of the curtain. No sirens screamed, no subways shook the walls and floor.

A raven called from high above the house and the water of the irrigation ditch tinkled as it passed her window. She breathed deeply, then remembered FISH hanging from Uncle Auggie's scale, tipping it at two and a half kilograms, measuring 58.4 centimeters, a little more than the height of the table.

"The all-time record!" she recalled Granddad shouting from the chair by the window. Uncle Augustus had hugged her and Paul and Alligator had smiled—half-heartedly.

"Spinner has won the medal," Granddad had said.

Uncle Augustus took a small gold fish from the top of the bookcase. "Champ of the fishing Shafters," he said, placed it in her hand, and hugged her.

Aunt Becky chuckled, Alligator shook his head and her father wrapped FISH in aluminum foil and put on his coat.

"I'm getting this monster to the taxidermist before he shrinks a fraction." He went out into the night. Spinner ran to her bedroom, closed the door, and buried her head in her pillow. She did not awaken until six.

The long sleep had not eased her anguish. The family fishing medal was on the bedside table to remind her of her father's deed. She pushed it under a book, took a deep breath, and stood up.

Spinner combed her hair until it gleamed, then lifted her hands to begin her morning dance exercises. Her arms ached and her legs felt as if they had needles in them. She gave up, dressed, and went into the living room. A fire in the Franklin stove cast yellow lights on the bearskin rug and the hand-hewn table and chairs. The front window framed the massive Teton mountains and illuminated the log walls of the large, cozy room.

"Morning, champ." Aunt Becky was up. Spinner tucked her shirt into her blue jeans and walked into the kitchen.

"Guess you showed them all," Aunt Becky said. "You won the Shafter fishing medal." She threw her head back and laughed. Wisps of gray hair tumbled around her sun-bronzed face, and her blue eyes crinkled and closed.

"I'm going home," Spinner said. "I hate to fish."

"Who says you have to fish? There's a rodeo in town and the wild strawberries are ripe enough to pick." Spinner moved closer. She felt comfortable with Aunt Becky, for she was a person of many persons. She sewed, cooked, gathered berries, chopped wood, built furniture, and stuck up for city folk. Two nights ago at the cookout, Spinner had slipped on a stone and dropped the steak on the ground. A guest's dog had grabbed it and run off with it before anyone could move. Aunt Becky had simply said: "Anyone for canned soup?"

"Aunt Becky," Spinner said, "FISH was beautiful and so old he must have been born when the river was born. I should have cut the line."

"You should have eaten him. That makes me feel better. Justifies the killing. After all, FISH ate little fish."

"He did?"

"Sure, and now that he's gone a little one can grow up and take his place."

Spinner imagined a tiny fry swimming into the empty hole and settling down to live among the spindly silver rocks and blue hollows. "But he won't be a cutthroat. They're mighty rare. Granddad said."

The door opened and Alligator came in smelling of the cedar walls of his cabin, which stood behind the main ranch house. The cabin was Alligator's private world. No one else ever went in it.

Al was barefoot despite the frost on the sage this summer morning. His pants were rolled up into disgusting baggy loops. Without even saying "good morning" he opened the refrigerator and took out a huge slice of watermelon.

"Want to go backpacking?" Spinner looked behind her to see to whom he was speaking. There was no one else in sight.

"If you're speaking to me," she said, "I'm going home."

"Up Ditch Creek to Crystal Creek, maybe to Desperation Peak?" Alligator bit into the melon and closed his eyes. "Hmmm," he said.

Spinner had never camped. She thought about the backcountry she had seen in Uncle Auggie's movies:

the sheer rocks and fields of snow. She recalled the storms and trumpeting winds. She shivered.

"Your fish," Alligator said. "He's a mystery, a portentous haunting mystery."

Spinner was surprised by so many words from Alligator.

"Where did he come from?" Alligator went on. "How did he get so big? What mysterious forces kept him alive when all other cutthroats died?" Alligator looked around as if someone might be listening.

She knew fishermen were secretive; her father even fibbed about where he caught fish, but Alligator was making a spy case of this. He was ridiculous.

"We'll follow his trail up Ditch Creek. I figure he was on his way home to spawn. If we find his spawning bed. . . ."

"We can find another and put him back in FISH's place?" Spinner asked and sat straight in her chair.

Alligator opened the door. He eyed her, then spit a stream of black seeds out over the porch steps. Spinner gasped and looked at Aunt Becky. Her back was turned. She had not seen her vulgar son. Alligator fired another volley.

"Al, stop that!" Aunt Becky did not turn around. "I see you."

"Spinner spit those seeds."

"Oh, I thought it was you, they jetted so fast. Guess Spinner's going home with all the family prizes. She can spit clear from the far side of the table and hit the bottom step of the porch."

"Humph," Alligator said and got to his feet. He wiped his mouth on his hand and licked it clean. Spinner looked at Aunt Becky but she was turning a pancake.

"Didn't see," Alligator said and rolled his eyes to the ceiling. He picked up an axe and went out the door.

Aunt Becky reached for her plate.

"He likes you," she said. "He never spits watermelon seeds for any but his best friends. And he never talks but to those whom he admires. Then he runs on and on like a river."

Spinner could not help smiling.

"Hi, champ." Uncle Augustus came into the kitchen and kissed her head. "Does that smile mean you're not angry anymore?"

"No, it doesn't," she said. "It simply means Alligator and I are going off to be ecological spies."

"Where are you going?" her father called from the living room.

"On a very dangerous journey into the backcountry,"

she said tartly, for she was still angry at him for keeping FISH and breaking his promise to her and her promise to FISH.

The door opened and Granddad came in carrying his rod. He was smiling.

"Been down to the river since dawn," he said. "Can't catch a big fish like Spinner's."

"You'll never catch a fish like that," her father said. "The river has changed since he was hatched." He clapped Aunt Becky on the shoulders. "I ordered a dark walnut plaque. . . ."

Spinner jumped up from the table, pushed past her father, and ran out the door. The mountains where she would be traveling looked formidable above the valley. She shivered, leaped over a cluster of purple lupine, and dashed behind the house. Alligator was chopping wood.

"When do we leave?" she asked.

"You want to go?" He tossed a log above his head, swung the axe, and split the log down the middle. Spinner whistled.

Suddenly she realized her cousin spoke not in words, but in deeds—a mouthful of watermelon seeds, a log split in midair. Well, then, she knew how to talk to *him*.

Spinner leaned, put one hand on the ground, lifted

her legs straight into the air, and turned a perfect cart-wheel. As she whirled to her feet, Alligator smiled.

"Good," he said. "I'm glad you want to go. Let's pack!" She trailed Alligator to the pump house. With a leap he grabbed the rafters and swung to the loft. Backpacks, sleeping bags, and tents rained down, then Al. He sprinted to Uncle Augustus' lab and gathered file cards and a bucket "for collecting specimens," he explained.

"We'll go light," Alligator said. "Eat off the land—fish, snakes, and yampa root. Then we can carry more sleuthing gear." He picked up a boxlike net.

Spinner clutched her stomach and ran to Aunt Becky, who reassured her that she did not have to eat snake if she did not want to. Then Aunt Becky put Spinner's pack on the floor and showed her how to roll her clothes and organize the pack. Into a side pocket she tucked a bar of sweet-scented English soap and into another a hand lens.

"I'm putting this in," Aunt Becky said of the lens, "because I know these Shafters. They spend most of their time looking at teeny things from the streams and this can be terribly dull unless you have a hand lens—then, it's wondrous." Her eyes creased mysteriously and Spinner wondered what could be so enthralling about things in a stream.

Finally, to Spinner's relief, Aunt Becky filled plastic bags with freeze-dried beef, peas and potatoes, packed packages of sauces, teas, and hot chocolates. When the last item was tucked away she filled the cracks with candy. Then Alligator and her father walked in the door.

"I know it's okay for Al to go backpacking," he said to Aunt Becky, "he's experienced, but Spinner's never been beyond Central Park."

"She'll be just fine," Aunt Becky said. "Out here in Jackson Hole backpacking is like going to the movies in New York. It's easy."

"Everyone does it," Alligator said as he put his pack on his knee and an arm in one strap. Then he let the pack rest on his back and put his other arm in the other strap. Spinner did likewise, staggered backward, regained her balance, and trod to the mirror in her bedroom. She fastened the hip belt.

"I'm a turtle," she said in surprise.

Aunt Becky came into her room, opened the closet, took down a broad-brimmed hat of straw, and put it on Spinner's head.

"The sun can cook your brains," she said. "You'll need this." Spinner looked at herself. She was very dramatic looking under the round white brim, her black hair flowing down.

"When it gets really hot," Aunt Becky went on, "tuck your hair up under the hat. It'll insulate your brains." She stepped back and folded her hands. "You look pretty."

Spinner threw her arms around her and hugged her as if she would never see her again. Then she tramped into the kitchen, trying not to stagger under the weight of the pack. She kissed her father out of habit. Reluctantly he opened the door and she strode off to meet Alligator. She did not look back for fear of changing her mind.

"Here I go, like it or not," she said to herself.

A bird flew overhead, the sagebrush crackled at her knees, and a little ground squirrel scampered into his hole.

"Al!" Uncle Augustus called from the irrigation ditch, where he was working. Alligator turned around. "You know you're going up into grizzly country?"

Alligator nodded.

"Take precautions."

He nodded again.

Spinner heard her father gasp—or had it been her own breath that had sounded like the wind in a tunnel?

3

THE TRAIL

The weight of the pack drove Spinner's feet hard against the stones and she stopped to rest and look back. Across the open flat the cabin looked no bigger than a cracker box, and under the enormous sky Aunt Becky's car was but a toy. The distance frightened her and she ran to catch up with Alligator.

"We are little planets adrift in space," she said.

"So be careful with yourself," he answered. "Don't waste even a breath. You've got only so much energy and resources."

She slowed down and thoughtfully stifled a desire for a candy bar. If the food ran out she would have to eat snake.

"We won't go far today," Al said, "just to the spot where you caught FISH. I am going to take a sample of the critters on the bottom of the river. I want to know what FISH was feeding on." They walked along quietly side by side.

"I figure FISH had just arrived in that hole," Al mused. "He must have been on his way up Ditch Creek to the backcountry to spawn." Alligator's boots crunched against the glacial till. "He *must* have just gotten there," he repeated, "or he would have been caught days ago."

"Why?" she snapped. "Just maybe I'm a good fisher. Why does everyone act as if my catching FISH was a freaky accident?"

At the edge of the second river bench they rested. Before them the Snake River wound between the gray sage and blue lodgepole pine forests. Above the pines the snow-clad mountains were white saw blades and the sky was a blue frame for the sun. Alligator smiled and jumped down the steep river bench like a goat, his feet together, his arms held high. At the bottom he glided around the cottonwood trees like a skier while Spinner struggled awkwardly down the slope. She gritted her teeth as she entered the grove. Insects buzzed in the hot afternoon sun, dust filled her nose. A twig slapped her cheek and stung like a bee. She covered her face with her hair and trudged on.

Alligator threw down his pack where Ditch Creek met the Snake. He unhitched his tent, opened it on a flat spot, and thrusting poles here, guy lines there, erected it in two minutes. Spinner waited for him to put up hers. He did not. Instead he took out the bottom-sampling net and started to the river.

"I guess," she called to Al, "that I build my house for myself?"

"Sure," he answered.

She slowly staked her tent and erected it on two poles. When she was done the roof sagged and the bottom was ripply, but she had done it herself. Spinner crawled in and peered out at the white-capped river. The walls made her feel cozy, but more than that, she had a joyous sense of achievement. She had conquered the wilderness; she had built a shelter.

Spinner was stretched out victoriously when Alligator peered in her door.

"Hmmm," he said, grinned at the sagging roof, and handed her a stack of 3 x 5 cards.

"I'm going to make a bottom count. That is, I'm going to count all the critters in about a decimeter squared on the bottom of the stream. When I call out the categories on these lists, check them off. I'm going to sample, count, and weigh this mass."

The cards read: date, locale, time, water temperature, vegetation, air temperature, oxygen content, wind, and water color. Spinner was aghast. Ecological spies were very scientific.

Alligator waded into Ditch Creek and put down the bottom-sampling net. He reached into two holes on either side and turned over the rocks and pebbles, silt and sand. "I'm washing all the creatures in this area into the trap," he said and pulled up the net. Holding it carefully, he crawled up on the bank.

"Now," he said, "let's see what the old giant was eating." He dumped the contents into one of his mess-kit pans. "Seven black-fly larvae, two mayfly larvae, nine caddis-fly larvae, and—that's all. Very strange. Such a big guy should have been living on crayfish and freshwater shrimp. But he wasn't because there aren't any. Make a note of that." Spinner was annoyed by his authoritative voice.

"What about the vegetation?" she snapped as she read the card. "Maybe he was eating trees."

"Trees do not grow underwater," Al said with exasperation. "Moss and algae do. Tiny creatures, like rotifers and amoebas, eat the moss and algae. Insect larvae eat the rotifers and amoebas. And the trout eat the larvae." Alligator tossed out the refuse, rinsed his pan in the creek, and sat down beside Spinner. Grasshoppers crackled around them. One alighted on Spinner's hand.

"Get it off!" she screamed. "Al, I'm scared. Get it off." Her mouth trembled.

"He won't hurt you." Alligator arose, leaped across the creek, and departed, leaving the grasshopper on her arm. She felt ill at the sight of the insect.

"I'm going to measure the depth and width of FISH's hole," Alligator called.

Pressing her lips, holding her breath, she flicked the grasshopper with her thumb and forefinger. It crackled, sailed over the wildflowers, and fell in the stream. "Oh, no," Spinner cried. "Don't drown." She jumped to her feet. The insect whirled in the current, then violently thrashed to a leaf. It boarded, sailed to a log, and leaped back to the bank.

"A tiny sailor!" she exclaimed. "Maybe I'll like this after all."

At FISH's hole Alligator took out a steel measuring tape and probed the wild pool. Spinner watched him thoughtfully. Her cold, grinning cousin might be harsh and "umphy," but he was efficient.

She decided to be efficient too. She picked up several stones, carried them to a level spot, and fashioned a small fireplace. Then she erected a forked stick and picked up Alligator's bucket, which he had made from

a coffee can that morning by stringing a piece of wire
through two holes punched in it. She filled the can with
water from the river and hung it on the stick. Then she
sat down and hugged her knees. Backpacking was Life.
She had erected a home and built a stone kitchen.

An osprey sailed overhead, a fish hawk her father
called it. "Where the fish hawk circles," he had said,
"look for fish."

Spinner stepped to the river and peered into the clear
water. There were no fish. Only a small leaf rode the
swift current. Suddenly the willows crackled and a fisherman appeared. He looked at the hole where FISH
had dwelled and apparently decided it was "all fished
out," for he turned and walked upstream.

Another crackle and two more fishermen appeared.
They, too, walked on. Spinner now understood why
FISH had been in that hole. Everyone *did* think it was
all fished out. They did not fish there. Yet her father
had. Why hadn't *he* caught FISH instead of the log?
Perhaps Alligator was right. FISH had just arrived
when she cast her fly. No, she mused, feeling the creature on her line once more, FISH knew the currents
and channels. He had lived in that hole a long time.

The bushes snapped again and Spinner looked into
the eyes of a young creature.

"A baby cow!" she exclaimed. "What are you doing

here?" Its nostrils expanded and it snorted loudly.
Spinner jumped backward, slid off the edge of the
bank, and fell a meter to the stream bed. Suddenly the
embankment shook and she looked up to see a mon-
strous cow leap over her head. She alighted about two
meters away, turned and faced her.

"*Yaaaaa!*" Alligator was screaming with all the
power of his lungs. The animal startled, glanced at Al,
then Spinner, then Al. Slowly, cautiously, she turned
around and trotted up Ditch Creek below the bank.
She bellowed to her calf. The baby lifted its saucer-
sized hoofs and wobbled along beside her.

"Dumb girl!" Alligator shouted. "Never get near a
baby moose. The mother will kill you with one strike
of her sharp hoofs." Alligator was trembling.

Spinner crawled slowly up the bank. She sat down
by her little fireplace and took out her matches.

"No fires!" he snapped. "If every fisher built a fire
there would be no more trees to hold the riverbank. We
cook on a gasoline stove."

Spinner pressed her arms to her body like a frightened bird. She had done everything wrong. It would
be best to sit still and stay out of trouble. She watched
Alligator prime his tin-can-sized stove. The flame flick-
ered, then settled down to a steady burn. Now she saw

an opportunity to be useful. She picked up the can of water and handed it to him.

"Where'd you get that water?"

"From the Snake."

"Don't use it. It's polluted from the lodge and camp-grounds upriver. Two million people up there every summer."

Spinner envisioned the vessel creeping with disease. She put it down and took her clean mess kit out of her pack. Al pointed to the spring in the cottonwood trees and she ran off to fill her pot. She returned and waited for orders.

Alligator did not give any. He dumped some freeze-dried meat and peas into the pot, let them boil for a long time, then opened an envelope of stroganoff sauce. He stirred in the mix and added dry potatoes.

"Chow," he announced and spooned her a portion. Spinner found to her relief that the food was deli-cious. She ate heartily and then stood up.

"You cooked, I'll wash the dishes," she said. Al gave a contemptuous laugh, jumped to the stream, and scrubbed the pot, his dish and spoon with sand. He did not offer to do hers, so she climbed down the bank, dipped her dish in the water, and then washed it with gravel.

The bushes snapped along the river as a fisherman returned.

"Any luck?" she heard Alligator ask.

"Trash fish," the man said, "three suckers and a Utah chub. Threw 'em back." He paused as Spinner joined them. "Don't know what's wrong with this river. Twenty years ago I could throw in a line and bring out big cutthroats as fast as I could cast . . . now, it's all junk fish. The river's gone sour."

The man tipped his hat and departed. Alligator looked·at the sun, took off his jacket and boots, and jumped into his sleeping bag in his clothes. Spinner was shocked. She crept into her tent and took out her nightgown. The sky darkened, a wind came up, and the cottonwoods sighed and clattered. Shivering in the cold air, she nevertheless performed her evening rituals. She undressed, creamed her face, brushed her hair one hundred times, and touched her toes fifty. Finally she lay down feeling clean and vastly superior to her uncouth cousin. She snuggled deeply in her sleeping bag. A twig snapped.

"Alligator!"

"Huh?"

"What about the moose? Will she come back and kill us?"

"Naw, she's a crepuscular creature. She's up in the

dawn and twilight. She's in bed when you're in bed."

Spinner rolled to her side and listened to the wind. Suddenly a coyote howled, its eerie voice sounding hysterical. She pulled her sleeping bag around her chin only to hear rocks rolling in the riverbed. They rumbled like distant kettledrums. The leaves had voices that scratched like claws. The wilderness was noisier than the city—and more terrifying.

Spinner could not sleep. Around midnight her lids fluttered. At last she was relaxed. An owl hooted. She slid to the bottom of her bag and clamped her hands over her ears.

About two o'clock in the morning, hot and exhausted, she crept to the top of the bag. People were laughing and talking somewhere. She sat up. The voices turned into the sound of water bubbling over the rocks in Ditch Creek.

Spinner lay down, wrapped her sweater around her ears, and waited for the sun. She was going back to Aunt Becky as soon as she could see the trail.

At five o'clock she dressed and put on her boots. Pans clinked. She parted the tent flaps to see Alligator stirring a pot of hot oatmeal. Crawling into the cool dawn, she gratefully accepted a cupful.

"We'll go up the Gros Ventre River today," Alligator said. "That's one of the rivers where the trout spawn

—mostly steelhead trout, but maybe we'll find some clues there."

Spinner cleaned her cup in the stream and packed. As she started up the trail she felt as if she were carrying the whole Teton Range, for lack of sleep had sapped her strength. She hesitated at the path to the cabin. The thought of Aunt Becky's cozy presence was overwhelming. She longed to run to her. Then the image of FISH gasping for water came back to mind. Taking a deep breath, Spinner followed Alligator up the stream bed.

Ditch Creek wound around Black Tail Butte and out across the alfalfa fields. The stream grew smaller and smaller. Where it slipped under the road it was a mere trickle and Spinner asked how FISH had swum through such low water. "His back would have been out all the way," she said.

"The ranchers are drawing off the water for irrigation now," Alligator answered. "This is a deep stream in early June when the fish come up to breed."

"So why was he in the Snake in July if he was on his way upstream to breed?"

"Hmmm," said Alligator.

"I just might have caught a fish no one else could catch."

"Umph," he grunted.

After crossing the sunny ranch land they entered a grove and walked through the soft, low light of aspen trees. Al sniffed.

"Elk." He sniffed again. "Migrating to the mountains."

Spinner sniffed, smelled a rancid odor, and quickened her pace. A magpie shrieked and she ran. At the edge of the grove she plunged through leathery willows and followed Alligator onto the shore of the Gros Ventre River. Spinner blinked in the bright sun.

The river was swift and wide and its shores were beaches of gravel. It sparkled through aspens and wildflowers. In the middle of the swift water a fish trap lay like a V-shaped dam. At an opening in the vortex stood three men in hip boots. They carried nets and buckets and worked swiftly catching fish swimming up through the V.

"Hi, Tom!" Alligator called. A young man with red hair and yellow beard waved, hoisted a bucket to his shoulder, and waded ashore. Tom looked from Al to Spinner and smiled.

"That's City Mouse, my cousin," Al said and gave her a shove. "What you doing, Tom?"

"Getting the last of the trout for eggs," he answered.

"Tom's with the Fish and Game Commission," Alligator said to Spinner. "They take the fertilized eggs, hatch and raise them in hatcheries until they're big enough to stock in the rivers."

"More survive in hatcheries than in the wild," Tom explained. "We protect the fry from predators and starvation. We feed them a rich diet that makes them grow fast, then put them in streams for the fishermen. Fishing's a big business out here. Millions are spent on it."

Alligator asked him if he had seen any cutthroats. Tom shook his head. "Not in about eight years. They're all gone from this area. Too bad. The cutthroat is the great native fish of the eastern slopes of the Rockies. Doesn't live anywhere else in the world! Beautiful fish."

Alligator opened his pack and took out crackers and a tube of peanut butter. He boiled water for tea, counted out forty raisins apiece, and told Spinner to sit down on a log and eat. She did—heartily.

Tom hoisted his bucket to the back of the Fish and Game truck and sat down on the log. With the air of a spy, Alligator pulled an envelope out of his pocket, opened, and took out a glass slide. He handed it to Tom.

"How old was the fish whose scale is on this mounting?" Tom scrutinized the pinhead-sized object that was the scale of a trout. Alligator had removed this one from beneath the dorsal fin of FISH with a knife.

Trout scales are tiny and buried in smooth skin. Tom took the slide to the back of the truck, brought out a microscope, and focused the lens. His bristly beard gyrated and he whistled.

"Cutthroat," he said. "A huge one! Where did you get him?"

"In the water," Alligator said without smiling, and Tom snickered.

"I should know better than to ask. No fisherman tells." He examined the rings enlarged by the microscope and counted them almost as if they were rings on a tree.

"He's seven," he said. "Zow, he really grew his second year. Wonder what he was feeding on. Did better than our hatchery-fed fish."

Alligator unpacked his bottom-sampling net and waded into the shallows of the river. Tom sat down beside Spinner and they watched Alligator.

"He won't get much of a food count," Tom said. "The Gros Ventre's silting up. The ditching and dyking for irrigation does it. Slows down the water, heats it up, and the little sand grains drop out. They fall on the stream critters and suffocate them . . . fish eggs die too. Less and less fish each year. If you want wild trout you've got to get into the mountains where the water is clear, cold, and swift."

Alligator came ashore. "Starvation diet here," he said and folded his net.

"The local climate's been changing in the last few years," Tom said. ". . . sort of a valley drought, mysterious because the next valley up gets rain. The drought affects the minerals in the water and the minerals affect the plants. The plants affect the fish. The fish affect the bears, and so on up the line to man. No fish, no licenses sold, no job for me."

Alligator studied his map, then the mountain. Presently he picked up his pack, signaled Tom good-bye, and beckoned Spinner. He struck out through the aspen for the dirt road that led into the backcountry.

The heat of the sun hammered Spinner's head and shoulders. She stopped, braided her hair, wound it on top of her head, and tucked it under Aunt Becky's hat. Instantly she felt cooler. Aunt Becky was right. Her hair was good insulation.

Spinner counted off two thousand steps before she looked back to check her progress. The Gros Ventre was a misty scarf in the distance, the fish trap mere toothpicks. A sense of wonder filled her. Her feet were remarkable transportation. They had carried her over the land without gasoline or tires. By simply placing one in front of the other she traveled through the woods, up stream beds, over meadows and rocks where neither car nor bike could go. Elated, Spinner trod on down the road. In the next valley she was surrounded by yellow and green hills of clay where the sage grew in hot, tight clumps.

A pickup truck rumbled around the bend and stopped.

"Want a lift?" Alligator recognized the driver, smiled and threw his pack in the back. He climbed into the cab and Spinner was left outside holding her bag. She waited for help, realized she was on her own, and heaved it aboard. She climbed into the truck. The dust was so dense she could barely make out the driver's face under his Western hat, but she did notice that his nose was broad and leathery and his mouth curled pleasantly upward.

"I'm Gunner," he said to Spinner. She smiled and licked the dust from her lips.

"Fishing?" he asked Al as he shifted into gear. The truck bounced down the rocky road.

"Yup, me and City Mouse here," Al said. Spinner straightened up and looked out the window.

"I'm Spinner, Alligator's cousin," she explained with forced politeness. Al growled and Gunner looked down at her and laughed.

"That's a good name for him," he said.

"Any cutthroats around?" Al asked. Gunner pushed

back his hat and said he had not seen any in years.

"But there are rainbows and steelheads in Crystal Creek," he said.

"Umph," said Al. "Would you drop us off there?" He unfolded a Geological Survey map and studied it, moving his finger up Crystal Creek to its source—a broken blue line among many brown lines.

"Right here," he said to Spinner, "we're going to find the first clue in the mystery story of FISH."

"What are the little brown lines?" Spinner asked.

"The height of the land. When the lines are close together they're precipices. Desperation Peak is marked thirty-five hundred meters. That's about fifteen hundred less than the Grand and fifteen hundred more than Mount Washington, and it's where we're going."

Spinner stared at the map, then at the mountains that surrounded them. She licked her dry lips and fought down her fears.

"Crystal Creek!" Gunner announced and stopped the truck. Spinner and Al climbed to the road, ran to the back of the truck, and retrieved their packs. Gunner rolled down the window.

"Take precautions," he called. "Grizzly country up there." Spinner stared at the formidable mountains and then down the road to home. She turned around to ask Gunner to take her back, but the truck pulled out, and she was committed to the blue-black valleys, the raw sun-baked hills, and the return of an endangered species.

A raven sat on a high pinnacle watching the valley with an ominous eye. Spinner was terrified of his hunched blackness and ran to the green trees along Crystal Creek. She sat down in the cool grass.

Where Crystal Creek meets the Gros Ventre the water collides in a wake, then speeds off toward the Snake. Spinner watched the water run back to Aunt Becky and longed to ride it home. She was about to set up her tent when Alligator pulled her to her feet and started down a wide trail.

"Old Indian fishing trail," he said. "We take it."

They strode out into the hot sun. Spinner pulled her hat over her forehead, shifted her pack, and followed Al. She could not keep up with him. She dropped farther and farther behind and for an hour she did not see him at all.

She had found her own pace, a slow, dogged step that did not tire her and so she tramped silently along at the foot of a high, sheer wall. She wound in and out of canyons, over dry washes, and down rock piles. Finally the trail cut across a grassy hill, and at the top of a mound she stopped.

Below lay Crystal Creek. It poured out of a cool

green forest and slid through the hot valley like a glass serpent. Flowers bordered it and birds skimmed over it. Spinner ran down the slope in glee. A tan dog slipped out of a clump of grass and trotted beside her, tail low, ears back. She whistled to him. He stopped. She stopped. The eyes of the animal were yellow and strange, and she realized he was not a dog at all but a coyote. She backed up. The coyote curled his lips in warning and Spinner took off like a frightened jack rabbit.

Legs flying, hat flopping behind on its string, Spinner covered the five hundred meters to Al in mere seconds.

"You look like a spooked horse," he said. "What's the matter?" She dropped her pack in the grass and glanced back. The hill was quiet and coyoteless.

"I'm a fast runner," she said. "I'm not scared. I'm not." Her knees trembled and her heart raced. "I just need some exercise." Alligator umphed and dumped the contents of the collecting net into his pan. Slowly Spinner unbraided her hair and let it fall over her shoulders. She felt its comfort. The day, she hoped, had ended.

"Get out a card and list this fish smorgasbord," Al said.

"Ask me nicely," she snapped.

The muscles in the back of Alligator's neck tightened. "There's no room for dancing-class etiquette in the wilderness," he said. "Help or cook."

Spinner blushed deeply. She had not yet even boiled water. She took out a card and pulled her aching body to the stream bank.

"We are near the trout spawning grounds," Alligator said. The very sound of his voice was irritating and she tried not to listen as he came wading toward her. "Here's a young steelhead trout, much smaller than those at the weir. The smaller they are the nearer their hatching grounds are." He glanced up at the peaks. "We can go on and find their grounds if you want to." Spinner heard that. She decided to speak in Alligatorese. She grabbed her pack, pulled it into a grove of dark fir trees, and collapsed on the ground.

At her feet Crystal Creek cascaded down a rock wall into a blue-black pool. Ferns and scarlet flowers rimmed it.

Spinner did not see the beauty. She stretched out, closed her eyes, and sensed only the coolness of the fir needles against her cheek. Soon she was rested enough to hear a pine sparrow. His song was a tinkle, like the wild water. She lay still, listening to the cool sounds.

"Dinner time," Alligator called. Spinner pushed to her elbows and watched Alligator put his fishing rod together. He whipped his line back and forth, then sent it speeding to the dark spot in the brook. A fish struck. Alligator set the hook in the fish, played him for a few minutes, and landed him with a swoop of his net. Spinner was determined to help cook tonight. She struggled to her knees, opened her pack and took out the gas stove. By the time she had it lit, Alligator had four beautiful rainbow trout. He umphed at her efforts but smiled.

"I'll make some potatoes," he said as he went to her pack, where the potatoes were stored. "Where's my coffee-can bucket?"

"I left it at Ditch Creek!" she gasped.

"City Mouse," he exploded, "I need that can! How can you be so stupid?" Spinner slumped into a heap, then slowly unlaced her boots. She loathed her superior, outdoorsy cousin. She wished she were in New York.

"Eat," he said presently, and passed her the pan of fish.

"No," she snapped. Her fingers had just enough strength to unroll her sleeping bag. Without even taking off her clothes or setting up her tent, she crawled in and lay down.

"Caught a Utah chub," she heard Al say with food in his mouth. "Trash fish have moved up here, too. The trout *are* doomed."

"What did you do with him?" Spinner lifted her weary head.

"Threw him back."

"All you hotshot fishermen!" She pushed herself painfully to her elbows. "You complain about the bad fishing, but you keep the trout and throw back the trash fish. Why don't you throw back the trout and eat the trash fish?"

Alligator lowered his tin plate and looked at her. "Spinner Shafter, you've just said something *very* important. That's good. Throw back the trout and eat the trash fish, or at least don't throw them back. By golly." He paused. "But how do we get fishermen to do *that*?"

Spinner could not believe she had been praised. Alligator's enthusiasm inspired her, and, as if out of nowhere, she remembered the delicious carp served with ginger and bean sauce in New York's Chinatown.

"The Chinese have a recipe for making trash fish good with ginger and bean sauce. I'll write it down. We'll print it and post it at all the campgrounds and fishing holes." Alligator nodded approvingly.

"Good idea. Umph," he said, and finished his meal in silence. He pitched his tent and crawled in.

The aches in Spinner's legs were more intense than any she had felt after dance practice. She tried to concentrate on relaxing, but the coming of night made her alert and tense. Presently she was all knotted up. On the pool a crowd of light and dark figures moved.

The pool surface broke into a thousand rings. Tiny dots appeared in the center of each ring. They exploded into gray stars that shot upward. The stars formed a hazy cloud and drifted to the shore. Terrified, Spinner lifted her head as the cloud approached. It was composed of hundreds of little eyes that were pinned on her. She was about to scream when she saw that the eyes belonged to gray flies. By fifties and hundreds the flies alighted on the leaves at the water's edge, trembled, and split open. Out of gray casings stepped larger flies with silver wing stubs and long scarf-like tails. Their bodies glowed red in the twilight. Each fly vibrated until its wings unfolded. Then they flew out over the pool, climbed upward, and dropped down in an undulating flight. Their long tails flowed gracefully. Some dipped so low they touched the water, and when they did so, the surface swirled and fish rose to take them.

Spinner called Al. He stuck his head out of his tent and saw the insect clouds.

"Mayfly hatch," he said. "They will emerge from casings, dance, mate, and die . . . all in one night. They have no mouths. They don't even eat. They just live, pass on their genetic code, and die."

The pool burst with circles of flies and fish, and Spinner, caught up in the strange excitement, pushed to her battered knees. Alligator joined her.

"In some such pool as this," he said, "FISH got his start. Perhaps in this very pool. Young trout need such a bloom of life to survive. In the water world the bigger you are the better your chances."

"Until a human catches you," Spinner said. "Then it's bad to be big."

4

THE MOUNTAIN

The loud rattle of a belted kingfisher awakened Spinner. She stretched and looked at her watch. Ten hours had passed since she had dropped off to sleep. Refreshed she rolled over and sat up. With each movement silver wings swirled up in clouds and settled back on her head and sleeping bag. Mayflies lay everywhere, their dance over, their lives done. Spinner felt as if she were in the graveyard of the stream. She leaped up and ran to the creek to rid herself of the eerie pall of death.

The pool where the dancers had emerged in the dusk was bright green in the dawn, and inviting. She slipped out of her slept-in clothes and plunged into the water. Its icy freshness took her breath and she yelled.

The cold water was almost as soft as air. It buoyed her high and she swam to the cascade as if she were kicking through foam.

Then she pulled up on a rock. Precisely at the water's edge a female mayfly flew from the bushes. The night was not yet done for her. She was starting last night's story again by laying eggs on the water as she dipped. The wild, cold brook would cradle the new dancers from egg to nymphhood and through the winter to next year's performance.

When the female had exhausted herself, she dropped and was swept into the current.

Spinner dried herself off on the rock with her towel, then crawled to the shore and dressed. She was lighting the stove when Al stuck his head out of his tent.

"The living room is swept," she said. "The beds are made and last night's party makers are dead."

Alligator stood in a pile of silent wings.

"Some party," he commented.

Spinner put her pot on the stove, and when the water boiled, stirred in the instant oatmeal. She served Al a generous cupful, which he took with some embarrassment.

"Umph," he mumbled and ate.

Anticipating the hot sun, Spinner braided her hair tightly and put it up on her head. She pulled Aunt Becky's hat over her ears and shouldered her pack. Alligator turned down his wool socks and stood up. He looked at Spinner.

"You look like another person without your hair," he observed and twisted his head the better to see her. "You look like a midge, I think."

She made a face that questioned.

"Nifty critter," Alligator answered. He squinted at the mountains, grunted, and led off.

The trail entered a dark forest of stately firs. Suddenly a red squirrel screamed. He flashed his tail and announced to his neighbor that Alligator and Spinner had entered the woods and were crossing squirrel property. This news was semaphored to the next squirrel who, with a flick of his tail and a chitter, passed it on to the next. As Spinner and Al walked, the forest clattered like a telegraph office relaying a crisis. Nesting birds became alarmed and sat low. A pine marten, the otter of the trees, flattened on a high limb. A Canada jay pressed its feathers to its body and peered down upon the pair. Like a professional spy, the jay tracked them to the edge of its range, then quietly turned back.

The forest ended. Alligator and Spinner were looking into a yellow-orange canyon. The wall had been carved by the wind and water into kings and queens and pawns. They were banded with red and gold layers of rock, and wore crowns of trees. Spinner looked at the sky expecting to see the giants who moved the geological chessmen.

"Crazy country," Alligator said as he took out his map and spread it on the ground.

"Umph," said Spinner.

"Here we leave the trail and bushwhack." He pointed to a snowfield in a high valley.

"We're headed up there." He placed his compass on the map where they stood and lined it up with the snowfield. Then he stood up. Holding the compass firmly against his chest, he turned his entire body until the needle was lined up with magnetic north.

"I'm facing northeast by east," he said. "So we line up this tree in front of us with that one on the hill, and walk on a beeline to the snowfield." He started off.

Spinner fell in behind him, occasionally looking back on the eerie geological carvings that now seemed to be people mocking her. She was glad to leave them, although the mountain ahead with its icy glacier and black rocks was not much more comforting.

For almost an hour they climbed upward through the stiff branches of the sagebrush. At last cool shade enveloped them and they were in a forest of spindle-shaped trees.

"Subalpine firs," Al said. "We're getting around thirty-five hundred meters. Nice up here." Dim speck-lets of sunlight filtered through dense needles. The wind sounded flute-like.

"Is this grizzly country?" Spinner whispered and rolled her eyes from limb to limb. Alligator grunted and pointed to a tree with four deep gashes in the bark.

"That," he said, "is grizzly-bear talk. It says: 'This is my land.' Claw writing, I call it." Spinner stepped closer to him.

"I'm scared," she confessed. Alligator gave her an exasperated glance.

"Grizzlies," he said, "sleep under the roots of trees on the northern slopes of the mountain all winter. In spring they migrate down to the yampa meadows to spend the summer. The bear who wrote on that tree is probably down in the flats digging up roots and catching trout in the streams. He would run if he saw you. In the backcountry grizzlies are more scared of you than you are of *them*."

"I don't believe *that*!" Spinner nervously took down her braids. She covered her eyes with them. Like an os-trich she felt that what she could not see would not hurt her, and presently she felt calmer. She uncovered her eyes and looked around. Al had disappeared. She spun around, ran down the hill, saw the grizzly mark, and sped back up. Her mouth went dry from fear, her hands dripped. She could not find the tree Al had selected as their next destination. She ran blindly, burst out of the forest, and came to a stop in front of a steep wall of rock.

There stood Al, studying it calmly, not even aware she had been lost among grizzly bears. She sat down, took out her canteen, and drank a long gulp of water. Alligator reached up, grabbed a crack above his head, and pulled himself to a ledge.

"I can't do that," she whispered hoarsely and hugged the rock. "I can't. I can't."

"About that grizzly," Al said, "they nap by day in the forests like the one behind you." Spinner reached up, clasped the crack, and fairly levitated. With one pull she was at Alligator's side.

"Umph," he said, raising his sun-bleached eyebrows.

The ledge was wide and Spinner walked unafraid for several decameters. Alligator pulled himself up to another ledge on the mountain. Spinner glanced down at the bear forest and climbed quickly to his side.

They faced a vast sheet of rock that sloped upward like a drawing table. Alligator simply strode up it, the waffled soles of his boots holding him to the surface.

He whooped with abominable cheerfulness as he skated upward. Spinner took a deep breath, gritted her teeth, and stepped out. Her mountain boot stuck and she ascended one foot after the other—holding, sticking, moving upward like a fly.

The wall was etched with cracks and in each crack was a little ecosystem. The dry ones supported hardy grasses that bent in the wind. The cold ones were icy deserts of fungi, and the wet ones were gardens of woodland starflowers and moss.

The slope steepened and Spinner dropped down to all fours. As she crawled, her boot loosened a stone. It snapped against the rock, bounced, and dropped into space. A long moment passed before it crashed at the bottom of the cliff. She trembled and glanced down. Far below, the fir forest stood. It was no bigger than the moss spires. She was so high that the valley of geological chessmen looked small enough to pick up and move.

Spinner was terrified. Slowly she crept toward Alligator.

"Where are we?" she asked.

"Heading northeast." He pointed to grooves in the surface of the rock. "The ancient glacier carved these north and south lines as it flowed. That's north," he pointed, "that's east, and we're traveling in between.

We'll soon be off this mountain. The present-day snowfield should be straight ahead."

Spinner climbed on without speaking or glancing down. Presently Al straightened up and looked back.

"A storm's coming," he said. His face paled a shade and Spinner felt her spine tingle.

"Come on," Al said, "don't like to be on exposed rock in a storm!"

Spinner hugged the wall, gathered her courage, and looked back. Black clouds had piled in the valley. Each had clawlike tendrils that seemed to be reaching for her. The lightning sparked like cat eyes, and she screamed, flattened herself to the wall, and closed her eyes. When she opened them, Alligator had climbed to a pinnacle and was scanning the mountainside.

"There's a krummholz of alpine fir in a crevice down there," he called, then jumped from the pinnacle and began to run. Spinner pressed against the wall, too frightened to move. A clap of thunder sounded, and she was catapulted after Alligator.

A snowflake struck her face. Another fell on her hand. The wind ripped her hat and, as she dropped to all fours, she was engulfed in snow.

Through the blizzard, Al whistled cheerfully in the distance.

"Why are you so happy?" she screamed in rage. "Because I'm going to die?" The blizzard whirled off, the air cleared, and there was Alligator almost beside her. He was pointing to a black animal with small ears and a mouselike face sitting on a ledge above their heads.

"Whistling marmot," he said. "He's the happy whistler. He wants to know who we are."

"Tell him we're fools," she said as she followed him trembling around a boulder.

She sat down. "My head is pounding," she complained.

"We're high," Al said, "real high. Marmots are dark above three thousand meters and that fellow was black. We must be about four thousand meters, high enough to give you altitude fever. Better rest."

Spinner leaned against the rock and nervously watched the storm climb out of the valley and cover the sun. Lightning danced on the pinnacle where Al had stood. It twirled and snapped like a rope of fire.

"Let's go!" Al ordered. The lightning was striking too near. Spinner held her head and stepped out on the wind-worn rock. An earsplitting thunder crack shook earth and sky.

"Hurry," Al called, and pressed against a rock to wait for her. When she caught up with him she was breathing hard.

"Take two short in-breaths and blow out through

your mouth," he ordered. "The air's thin up here, not much oxygen. You've got to breathe fully and quickly or you'll pass out." Spinner followed his directions and he turned and darted on. She ran too. The storm enveloped them. Snow swirled, rain pelted, and she slipped. With a cry she dug in her fingers and knees, stopped herself, and regained her footing.

"Want me to take your pack?" Al asked. She looked into his worried eyes, shook her head, and got ready to run for the krummholz. Suddenly Alligator's mouth lit up like a pumpkin head's and his eyes flashed. His great sheath of hair stood up straight in the air. She screamed.

"I'm okay," she heard him say before the thunder boomed. "Are you?" Spinner was not certain. Surely she was dead.

Silence followed the cannonade. She peered around. The mountain was still there, the flowers still bloomed in the cracks. Her hands were cold and her legs ached, but she was very much alive. She breathed deeply. Ozone from the lightning filled her lungs.

"Let's go!" Alligator said and dashed across the rock face. He dove into the krummholz as the wind lashed the dense cluster of trees. Spinner plunged after him, crept under the limbs, and collapsed in a heap.

Presently she looked around. The mountain was

barely visible through the mat of short needles that covered the twigs of the trees. Gratefully she touched the firs that fended off violence and protected her from the storm.

"Put on your poncho," Alligator said. "It's going to pour."

She struggled into the mass of nylon as the krummholz lit up, thunder pealed, and the rain blazed down. The drumming and flashing became a continuous explosion.

"Al," Spinner whispered, "I'm sorry I lost your bucket."

"Umph," he grunted, "don't say anything you'll regret because you're not going to die." His eyes flashed in lightning.

She umphed, sat still, and dropped her head on her knees. Home came to mind. Her mother was making a salad for lunch, and Pip, the cat, was on top of the refrigerator. Down the block the Roundelay Dancers were eating yogurt and stretching at the barre, and her best friend, Amanda, was listening to tapes. None of these people, she realized, was the least bit aware that she was out on a mountain about to be struck by lightning. It seemed incredible that she would die and no one would know.

"Watch it!" Alligator's voice startled her and she

looked up as the krummholz blazed with light and the deep and dreadful kettledrums of thunder rolled. The hairs on her arms rose like bristles.

"Close," Alligator said through the sizzling sound of rain. He reached into his pack and passed her a candy bar. The rain changed to snow, ozone filled her lungs, and her breath came more easily. As she inhaled the oxygen-rich air her headache vanished.

The next lightning strike was less forceful, the thunder but a hand clap.

"The storm's moving off," Alligator said and leaned his head against a gnarled limb, closed his eyes, and in a moment was snoring. Spinner relaxed. If Alligator could sleep the crisis must be past. She listened to the wind piping oboe-like sounds over the top of the mountain and dropped off to sleep too.

The sun came out. Spinner awoke, wriggled out through the limbs, and cheered. The mountain was white with snow and every crystal was sparkling with a hundred lights.

"Al," she called. "Al, wake up. Come see this summer-winter day."

He crept out of the matted trees, looked around, and yawned. "Up here," he said, "with the starflowers and krummholzes, summer is but one day in mid-July."

A rodent ran past the dwarf trees carrying a bluebell.

"See," Alligator said, "the little rock rabbit, or coney, is just picking the bluebells. They're April flowers down below." The soft-eyed animal hesitated at the sound of Al's voice, then dashed off with its prize.

"They dry flowers in the rocks," Al said, "and store them in bins for the winter. Nice, isn't it?" He picked up his pack.

The hot sun quickly melted the snow and the rocks became slippery. Spinner followed Alligator cautiously around the mountain. At the far side he paused at the top of a steep slide.

"There," he said pointing straight down, "is camp."

Almost one hundred and fifty meters below, a grove of tall trees stood in a rocky ravine. The sound of falling water was alluring. The calls of birds enticed. Alligator whooped, put two feet together, and leaped from rock to rock as he descended. He whistled his fishing song as he went down the mountain.

Before Spinner could crawl a meter, Alligator was at the bottom. Nevertheless she did not hurry. She lowered herself from one boulder to the next as she went down the rugged ladder of the mountain.

Three meters above the tops of the trees her feet struck a slide of sandlike talus. She turned around, sat down, and slid into camp on her seat. A porcelain-white glacier lily bloomed by her hand and her boots were buried in ferns. Jade-green grass touched her cheek and orange, yellow, and red flowers were splattered all around her.

"I must have been struck by lightning," she said. "This is heaven."

Spinner squirmed out of her pack, stood up, and followed the sound of falling water through the trees. She pushed back a bush. A white cascade dropped like a glorious scarf from the high valley above.

In its spray zone the wet rocks nourished ferns and mosses. Delicate flowers shone like blue and green crystals in the eternal mist and the outer edge was gold. A rainbow arched across the falls. Spinner waded into the water and sat down on a rock. Spray and white thunder enveloped her. She was in the soul of the waterfall.

Suddenly a small gray bird popped up out of the water. It looked like a wren but it floated like a cork. With a flip of its tail it went under. Spinner leaned over. The bird was on the bottom of a clear green pool. Spinner rubbed her eyes. The bird surfaced, docked at a rock, and climbed out of the water. There it bobbed up and down like a mechanical toy, spread its wings, and flew into the waterfall.

"Oh, no," she cried and ran to look for the dead body of the bird where the fall crashed on the rocks. Bells chimed and she turned around. The bird was singing safely on a rock at the edge of the cascade.

Alligator joined her, fishing rod in his hand.

"Am I lightning struck?" she asked. "I see a bird flying in water."

"You're okay, that's a water ouzel." He grinned. "He's good news. He lives in fast, wild water where cutthroats dwell." Alligator pointed across the stream. Another ouzel floated in and out of the splash at the bottom of the falls.

She dove under and Spinner could see her walking on the bottom of the stream pumping her wings. She shot her head swiftly among the stones. "She's pecking," she said.

"Eating nymphs and midges—trout food," Alligator explained. "Where dippers dip, trout nip." Al whipped his line out and dropped a fly in a pool near the bird.

"The water ouzel winters downstream near our house," he said. "It nests in the high country. Sing and dance when you see an ouzel, it means wildness and clean water."

The two birds surfaced, bobbed over the water, and separated. The female picked up a billful of moss, flew up and over the waterfall to her nest on the canyon wall. The male winged to a rock in the spray, threw back his head, and chimed out a song with bell-like tones. Then he flew into an air pocket behind the thundering cascade. Here he rested without fear. The waterfall was his protector. Spinner sat down on a boulder and swirled her feet in the clear water.

"Alligator!" He turned around. "There's a dance team of fish down here." Al leaped from rock to boulder and dropped to his knees at her side. The fish were blue-backed and densely spotted.

"Cutthroats," he said, and got on his stomach. The fish had arranged themselves in a diamond shape, all spaced precisely the same distance apart. They waved their tails in unison. All were about eight centimeters long, except for the one at the head of the triangle. He was much longer.

"Umph," said Alligator. "Ziz!" He scratched his head, and Spinner, suspecting that he was about to catch a fish and eat it, promptly named the leader.

"That's BUGS," she said. Now the fish was a person and Alligator would not catch a person. "He's the fellow we're looking for," she said. "BUGS will take FISH's place."

Alligator did not seem to hear; he was too preoccupied with fish-watching. Spinner got down on her stomach and peered into the pool too. The sunlight, shining through the water, duplicated the currents on the bottom of the stream. Spinner could see that each fish hung where the current bent as it flowed off the fish ahead.

"The bend holds them in place," Alligator said. "They don't have to fight the current. That's neat; hydromechanics makes the diamond spacing."

He caught a stonefly and threw it on the water. BUGS snatched it. The other fish fanned and waited. He tossed another and another. BUGS ate until satisfied, then the fish behind ate.

"BUGS is dominant," Alligator said. "He's the top fish of the team. That's why he's bigger. Gets first snap at floating insects."

Spinner rocked back on her heels. "If that's so, we need to take this whole dance team to Ditch Creek," she said. "If we just take BUGS he might get on the end of a diamond and die."

Alligator agreed that they could not take one fish. "But there's another answer here," he said. "I don't know what it is, but maybe if we just stare hard we'll think of it." He stared.

Spinner stared and listened. The stream whispered off through the dark alpine fir forest, fell over a ledge somewhere, and rushed off to a distant destination. She cocked her head and looked at the sun.

"If Crystal Creek joins the Gros Ventre, which is west of us," she said, "then why is it flowing east?"

Al listened. He looked at the stream, then at the sun, and finally at Spinner. "You're right. This can't be Crystal Creek!" He got up and looked around in puzzlement. "It *is* flowing the wrong way. We've climbed down into some other valley."

He looked at the landmarks—two peaks, a sheer cliff, timberline—then hopped to shore and took out his map. He found none of these features and realized they had gone farther on the stone mountain than he had thought.

"We're off the map," he said. He did not seem the least bit worried, so Spinner took her cue from him. She shrugged and picked up the bottom-sampling net. She splashed into the stream and waded to the foot of the waterfall. There she sank the net in the pounding water, put her hands through the two holes, and carefully turned over the rocks. With each move she dislodged waterfall creatures. They tumbled over her hands and were trapped in the net.

As she worked, she discovered that the creatures did not live under the rocks, where it was protected and safe, but in the full rush of the water. This seemed incredible. How could animals dwell in the swift violence of a waterfall? She stuck her hand under the white cascade and was almost knocked down by its power.

Spinner carried the net ashore and emptied it in Alligator's frying pan. Her eyes widened in astonishment as a host of zany beasts crept out of the debris. Most were small, about a millimeter long. All bristled with mechanical devices like grapples and hooks. She called Alligator. He examined the catch.

"Black and stonefly larvae mostly," he said. "And there's one midge."

"Let me see *that,* since I look like one." Spinner darted to her pack to get out the hand lens, and Alligator put the midge on her palm. She peered through the glass. In the circle of magnification sat a glistening creature. It was many-jointed and dark, and on its head was a structure that looked like a broad-rimmed hat.

"Yes, that's me, and it even has flowing hair." She giggled and watched the creature tumble on its back. On each segment of its belly were suction disks for holding the midge to stones. In the center of each sucker was a plug.

"That plug is raised and lowered by muscles," Al said when she mentioned it. "When the plug is in, a vacuum is created and the creature sticks in the torrent. In case that fails," he went on, "cement glands around each sucker exude a secretion . . . glue; so it's plugged *and* glued to the rock. And, in case they both fail, tiny hairs clamp down to prevent water from seeping in and breaking the vacuum. In this manner the midge lives

in the rapids and in the terrible boom of the waterfall."

Spinner put the Thomas Edison back in the freshet.
Instantly it stuck to a rock with all its inventions, then
it pulled a plug, moved the sucker forward, and re-
planted it. Slowly, carefully, it moved up the torrent.

"You think that's neat, look at this," Alligator said,
and put a mayfly nymph in her hand. Through the
hand lens she could see that the creature had a hook on
each foot and grapples all along its gills. These held it
to stones in the fast, wild water. Huge black eyes on the
back of its head looked up and forward at the same
time. Alligator said the insect had invented two-way
eyes because it lived on the bottom of streams and
needed to watch upward for enemies and forward for
food. More wonderful than that, he said, the mayfly
of the rapids carried its own collecting bucket to catch
its plankton food. Hairy front legs and bewhiskered
mouth parts trapped the microscopic life of the water.

"You have a caddisworm," Alligator said, peering
back into the pan. "Net-builder type." Under the hand
lens Spinner could see a perfect little net with warp and
woof and beside it a little creature. The net strained
food from the rushing water and the creature dipped
into it and ate.

The green-gold film, in the pan, Al told her, was a

cluster of one-celled animals—desmids and diatoms. "That's what the caddis fly nets," he said. Also in the pan were green tufts of algae, a snail who mowed the algae, and a leech who sucked the fluids of the snail.

"And here's a water penny." Al picked up a copper-colored disk. The animal was flat, round, and fringed with hooklike hairs. He put the water penny in the current. Its hairs clasped a stone and the flow pounded it tighter and tighter to its mooring. Spinner was enchanted.

"Look here." Alligator stared at the stream bank. "Here's Baetis, the diving-bell queen, who lives in the quiet edges of wild streams." Spinner flopped on her stomach and looked down on a fly with large iridescent eyes that glimmered like miniature lanterns.

"Baetis goes down to the bottom of the stream in an air bubble," Alligator said and poked a grass blade at her. The alarmed fly lifted her wings, caught air under them, and dove to the bottom. The air created a silver bell. Safely removed from her gargantuan enemies, she breathed and waited for their shadows to pass.

Alligator plunged into the streams and splashed off toward the waterfall. With a hoot he slipped behind it. Spinner heard him sing and holler. Captivated, she held her breath, and sidled to him. She opened her eyes. She was in the pocket behind the overshoot. She breathed air. Founts and spurtles fell, the water ouzel preened on a rock above her head, and small things crept up the carpet of water mosses on the rock wall. The barrier of falling water made a secret castle. The downrush sheltered unique creatures of glitter and bubble. The kingdom behind the waterfall was awesome.

"We're in the most delicate zone of the mountain," Al shouted. "Here the small clamberers hide."

He pointed to a creature on the rocky wall.

"There's another species of midge"—his hand moved on—"and here's a caddisworm and a beetle."

For a long while Spinner stood in the gleam and roar, tranquilized by the strange world and the endless cannonade.

Finally she stuck her head through a part in the water. There was the sunlight. A flycatcher bird was catching insects that were bursting out of the waterfall.

Alligator poked his head out of the niagara and looked at the insects too.

"The bloom of the waterfall midge," he said and snatched one of the net-veined flies almost as swiftly as the bird.

"How do you know all these creatures?" she yelled.

"From fishing," he shouted. "To catch fish, you find out what insects they're eating, and copy them to make a fly to cast."

Spinner went back under the falls and sidled ashore. In an eddy at the stream's edge a few creatures were perched on the surface of the water. One was the whirligig. Spinner reached for it and the beetle wheeled off in darts and circles, steering a zany course through the rocks. It used a guidance system like a ship's wake that it made by drumming its feet on the water. The waves struck objects, bounced back, and informed the whirligig of the whereabouts of stones, leaves, food, and enemies.

Having failed to catch the whirligig, Spinner reached for a water strider. It dropped a bit of camphorlike chemical on the water. The oil reduced the tension and formed a wave. The wave shot the insect across the surface. Spinner sat down on the shore. The stream was fecund with wild geniuses, creatures that traveled on plugs, walked on water, changed shape, size, and habits. She leaned closer to the water, the better to see the ingenious animals. Her eyes flashed to some polished pebbles.

"There are golden beads down here," she said, reached for her cup, and scooped them up from between the clean stones. She showed them to Alligator.

"Ziz!" he exclaimed. "Cutthroat eggs. That's the answer we've been looking for! I've got it! We don't take a fish to Ditch Creek, but eggs to Crystal Creek. The young cutthroats will hatch, grow, and move down to the Snake naturally via the Gros Ventre." He took out his hand lens. "Eyed eggs, they're about twenty days old—still within the egg sac. In sixteen days they'll hatch and start toward the Snake. That's perfect."

Spinner peered at the "eyed eggs" through the magnifier. In each bauble thrashed a slender creature with large dark eyes, black intestinal track, and tiny heart. The hearts beat swiftly.

"They're dying," she cried and impulsively threw them into the pool. The current carried them away.

"Don't!" Al shouted. "I want them!" He growled at her, jumped into the stream, and began a search for the redd-eggs, the name of a trout nest.

After a long hunt he came ashore empty-handed. He took out a knife, dug lily bulbs, and plopped them into a bucket. He lit the stove. Spinner was terrified. Next he would catch a snake.

She slipped behind a tree, set up her tent, and crawled in. When her door was zipped she took out a candy bar and waited in agony for Al to unzip the flap and dangle a snake before her. An hour passed, and when he did not, she relaxed, brushed her hair, and lay down. She reached into a side pocket and counted the candy Aunt Becky had given her. She had enough to survive another night.

"Hey, Spinner! Dinner!" Al called. She envisioned snake.

"I'm not hungry."

"I threw back the trout and kept some trash fish—a mess of little minnows. We can experiment with them. Help me spice them up with something."

Spinner slowly unzipped her tent flap and peered out. No snake coiled from Al's fingers. Instead, he was kneeling over the little stove with his pot. Beside him lay leaves, bulbs, and a cluster of tiny fish he had cleaned. She joined him eagerly.

"I've got some balsamroot leaves," he said. "It's good tasty forage for mountain sheep, so it ought to be good for us." Spinner smelled a large silvery leaf. Its spicy pinelike odor suggested thyme and bayberry. She smiled, put the fish on several leaves, and seasoned them with salt and pepper. Al walked along the stream and picked a plant. "Blue-flowered lettuce or chickory," he said. "Want to try it for spice?" She nodded. Carefully she wrapped everything in the balsamroot leaves, put them in her pot, and covered it with a lid.

"Now for the roots and bulbs," Al said, licking his chops at the sight of the pot.

They worked together quietly, peeling bulbs, seasoning, and tasting. Finally the "wild" dinner was ready to be served. Spinner put fern leaves on a rock, a blue gentian beside Al's dinner bucket, and dished out the fish and vegetables. Carefully she tasted her meal, then glanced up at Alligator. He was looking at her.

"Sensational!" they said simultaneously.

Long after dark, Spinner lay in her sleeping bag thinking about the dinner. "The fish could have used a bit of ginger," she called out to Alligator. "And a little more chicory."

Al did not hear. He was hanging the food bags in a tree where the grizzlies could not reach them.

5

CUTTHROATS

Spinner awoke to the song of the ouzel and the freshness of splashing water. She lifted her head and peered out her tent door. Dew sparkled on ferns and the dawn light made pale rainbows in the waterfall. She moved to get up. Every muscle was stiff from climbing. "Oh," she cried, and rolled back on her sleeping bag.

Muffled scratchings and clinks told her Alligator was up.

"Spinner," he called. "I don't know what stream we are on, but I do know there are cutthroats downstream . . . else how would those eggs get here?"

"Umph," she said.

"Let's follow the stream down mountain and find the adults."

Spinner had not undressed again last night. She brushed her hair, and with great pain crawled out of her tent and limped to the stove, where Al was cooking breakfast. He seemed cheerful. Perhaps their wilderness dinner had soothed his anger. He seemed to have forgiven her for throwing back the eggs.

"Cutthroats," he said, thinking out loud, "spawn in wild streams like this. As they grow they move downstream to deeper and deeper water. Finally they reach the big rivers. Then"—he stabbed the oatmeal to punctuate his thoughts—"then, when they are mature, they smell the salts and minerals of the streams in which they were born and return to lay their eggs."

Spinner left Alligator to his musings, walked to the stream, and stepped in the water.

Near the bank, where the current was quiet, was a mass of soft gelatin.

"Cutthroat eggs. Cutthroat eggs," she screamed excitedly. He dashed to the shore.

"Frog eggs," he grunted, and turned to go back. His eyes caught a gleam beyond Spinner and he jumped into the water.

"Cutthroat eggs," he cried triumphantly.

Spinner ran ashore, grabbed the collecting bucket,

and dashed back. Together they eased the eggs into the container, and then, heads touching, they both stared into the bucket. Some eggs were quite large, others small.

"Looks like a few fish start off life bigger than others," Al said. "FISH was probably a big egg, a big hatchling, a big fish."

Spinner pushed back her hair.

"That's it," she said, "the mystery's solved! That's why FISH was so big. He had a head start. And he stayed big by getting to the top of the diamond and eating first." She smiled. "Now all we need to do is put the eggs in Crystal Creek and our mission is done."

Alligator hoisted the bucket to his shoulder and told Spinner to wait while he went to Crystal Creek and planted the eggs.

"Then," he said, "we'll follow this stream to the cutthroat river." His eyes danced with anticipation. "Somewhere there are some more big cutthroats."

Alligator loaded his gear, asked Spinner to watch his pack, and climbed up the talus slope with the bucket. When she heard him tumble rocks far up the mountain, she crawled back into her tent and lay down. She was grateful for the respite from any more hiking.

Sometime later Spinner was awakened by the crack of a limb. She sat up, pulled her bag around her, and listened. Footsteps were coming toward her along the stream. "Bear," she thought. Terror seized her. Then through the air vent she saw a bulky man with a fishing rod. He was peering into the pool at the foot of the waterfall. He turned, saw her tent, and quickly came toward her. There was no telephone to dial the police, no one to hear her scream. She clutched her heavy mountain boot and was flailing it when the man looked through the parted flaps.

"Oh," he said at the sight of her all alone, "what are you doing here?"

"I'm camping with my—father," she added quickly, her city survival techniques coming swiftly to her defense.

"Fishing?" The man sounded threatened and she remembered how competitive fishermen could be about their fishing holes. With sudden wiliness she announced that she and her father were bird-watchers. The man seemed relieved, glanced at Alligator's pack, and went back to the stream to fish.

Spinner huddled in her tent. From time to time she looked out at the rocky face of the mountain through the air vent. The sun was past the noon hour and was starting down the western sky. Alligator was not back. He had said he would only be gone two hours; at least four had passed and still there was no sight of him. A terrible thought seized her. Alligator was dead at the bottom of the cliff.

Spinner put on her boots, rolled up her sleeping bag and tent, stuffed pots and pans into her pack, and picked up Al's pack. The grasses rustled and a robust girl in a blue sweater and faded jeans walked into the grove.

"Hello," Spinner said to the freckle-faced stranger.

"Call me Maude Marsh," she answered and flashed a grin that displayed sharp, pointed teeth. "That's my dad, Reston." She pointed to the fisherman. Then with deliberate movements she scratched her stomach, took a wide stance, and folded her arms on her chest. Maude was a threatening sight. Spinner dropped Al's pack and made a fist.

"Campin' with someone?" Maude asked.

"My dad."

Maude studied Spinner through splintery eyes. Her father joined her and folded his arms also. They were a formidable pair and Spinner was thoroughly frightened.

"They're bird-watchers," the man said. Maude ignored him. "You ain't with your dad. You're with a kid. Some boy. I can tell."

Spinner backed away.

"She is, Dad," Maude said. "High-school track

sticker on his pack." She kicked it. Mr. Marsh turned his back and walked to the stream. With a flip of his wrist he cast his line into Bugs' hole. Anxiously Spinner watched him; those fish must get back to the big river where their parents grew up. She wanted to stop him, but was too frightened to speak.

"We're up here on a secret," Maude said abruptly. "A big one. A big, big one." She grinned slyly and took a candy bar from her pocket. Spinner shifted her pack and tightened her hip belt.

Maude asked her why she didn't want to know what the secret was.

"Because it's a secret," Spinner answered, "I presume you won't tell me."

"Well, you're wrong," Maude said. "I will, 'cause you're a bird-watcher. A dude came to the house two nights ago. Since you're not a fisherman you have to know this: fishermen fib about where they catch fish and how big they are."

Spinner glanced nervously up the mountain.

"Well, this dude came to my dad. My dad's a taxidermist. The dude had the biggest cutthroat trout ever. No one has caught one in these parts for ten years, much less one that big." Spinner's fears were replaced by amazement. She listened closely.

"And, get this: that dude told my dad he had caught

the fish in the Snake River near the ferry. That's the first lie."

"Why is that a lie?" Spinner asked innocently.

Maude chewed her candy, swallowed, and shifted her weight to one foot. "Why is that a lie? Listen to this. As Dad prepared the fish, his knife hit a metal tag almost completely buried under the skin!"

"A tag?"

"Yeah, one that the Fish and Game Commission had put on."

"So?" Spinner tried to be casual as Maude told how her father had then phoned the Fish and Game Commission for data on TROUT 762–AO—FISH. The official reported that 762–AO had been one of a thousand fingerlings tagged in Desperation Creek four years before in the hope of learning where the last of the cutthroats traveled and grew up.

"Is that why you're here?" Spinner asked nonchalantly.

"That huge cutthroat was caught right here, and we're here to catch its mammoth brothers and sisters. Or, Yes, if you want a simple answer."

Spinner shifted her pack and backed toward the mountain.

"Maudie!" shouted Mr. Marsh. "Get my net and bucket. I've found some little cutthroats. We'll stock our creek with 'em." Maude started off to obey her father, then glanced back at Spinner.

"Wait for me," she called.

Spinner wanted to scream, "Leave the cutthroats alone," but her concern for Alligator was greater than her concern for the fish. Al was bleeding to death in some dark canyon and she must find him. She picked up his pack and slowly, awkwardly, made her way up the slide to the sheer face of the mountain.

A rock slipped above her. Spinner flattened herself to the wall and looked up in terror. A mountain sheep, antlers curled like stone circles, stood but meters away.

"Oh," she said, "you scared me. Have you seen Al, my beloved cousin?"

The animal twitched its nostrils, looked around and sprinted to the top of a boulder. There, seeing danger, he put his feet together and rocketed out of sight. Al came around the boulder! He leaned across the rough surface and grinned down at her.

"Here's your beloved cousin!" He grimaced smugly.

"Baaaah," Spinner screamed, "Bah!" She turned her back.

"You look like a moving van," Al shouted. "What are you doing with all those packs?" She did not answer. How, she thought, could that reptile be Aunt

Becky's son? He was loathsome, scaly, noisy, and insensitive. She kicked a rock, pulled her hair over her face to express contempt in Alligatorese, and sat down on his pack. He jumped lightly to her side.

"The eggs are planted," he said. "FISH has been returned to the hole at Ditch Creek and the Snake."

With a triumphant whoop, Al snatched his pack right out from under her and started down the mountain. Spinner tumbled onto the rocks, where she determined never to move again. But Al did not look back and her resolution was lost on herself. She trailed him on her fanny down the talus to the grove. She had a trump card yet to play.

"By the way," she said carving her words carefully. "This is Desperation Creek." Alligator turned around in surprise.

"How do you know?"

Spinner longed to tell him that she had figured it out on *his* map, but she could not. Out blurted the story of TROUT 762–AO, the taxidermist, and his daughter.

Alligator listened like a stunned dragon to every detail, including Maude's mission to get the collecting bucket for capturing Bugs. Then he raced to the rocks at the bottom of the waterfall. The pool where Bugs and the other young cutthroats had dwelled had been disturbed.

"He *did* take them," he yelled over the boom of the water.

"Oh no!" Spinner cried.

She felt a lump of sadness rising inside her. It burned her throat and she crept over to Alligator and stared at the empty pool. The mountain was bleaker for the passing of the rare fish.

Alligator studied the sun and water, adjusted his pack, and beckoned Spinner. She tagged behind as he strode downstream along the flower-trimmed edges of Desperation Creek. The blue gentians colored the banks that were punctuated with white saxifrage blooms. They walked in silence.

Presently the creek cut into rock and roared off in a canyon. "We have to leave the water's edge here," Alligator said, and climbed to the top of the gorge.

They crawled over fallen logs and wound between trees, following the sound of wild water and occasionally the mysterious wisdom of Al's compass.

The forest became more dense, the footing more difficult. Only a few shafts of sunlight pierced the canopy, so Al picked a course deep in the forest where the walking was easier. After a kilometer or two they came back to the creek. The white highway up which the cutthroats had swum to their breeding grounds still lay far down in the gorge. Spinner paused and

looked down into the dark chasm. Spray exploded
from rocks and rainbows arched over riffles and cas-
cades.

"Look!" Spinner yelled. "Two people down there!
It's the Marshes! They're stuck!"

The man and his daughter stood on a narrow ledge
above the roaring water, their fingers clenching the
cracks of the canyon wall.

"They can't go up or down," Alligator said. "And
they can't stand there very long. If they fall they'll be
killed." He made a quick assessment of the canyon,
told Spinner to follow him, and climbed down a wide
crevice that angled along the rock face. Spinner hesitated, then crept into the crack. She eased down. When
the angle steepened, she turned on her stomach and
reached for the next ledge with her feet. Holding on
tightly, she dangled over the roaring chasm. Her fingers slipped. Miraculously Alligator sensed her danger,
grabbed an ankle, and guided her foot to a rock. She
stood firmly, rested for a moment, then eased down to
the wide ledge where he stood. From this point she
could see the frightened expression on Maude's face.
Her eyes rolled wildly and her freckles were dark on
pallid cheeks. Al took off his pack, unzipped the bottom pocket, and unrolled his climbing rope.

"I'll rappel to them," he shouted to her over the bombilating roar of water. Then he tied the line twice around a jutting rock and tested it. "When I signal, untie the rope and drop it down to me. I'll lower them on the rope to the water's edge. They can get out over the rocks there."

"How will you get back up?"

He mimicked a monkey climbing, then took the rope between his legs and wrapped the line over his shoulder and down across his chest. Taking a firm hold, he backed off the ledge and let himself down in leaps and swings to a rock shelf about a meter below the Marshes. He signaled Spinner to drop the rope.

The rope fell away. Spinner was alone on the side of the precipice unable to go up or down herself. She tried not to think about that. Somehow Alligator would get back to her. He would.

Al reached up and helped Mr. Marsh and Maude to the ledge he was on. They were safe. Quickly he wrapped the line around a rock and then around Maude. With explanatory gestures he showed her how to rappel off the cliff. Maude backed to the edge, looked down, and shook her head violently. Al thrust his fist at her. Her face contorted and she froze on the cliff. In desperation Al kicked her boots until there was no place to go but down. She stepped off, spun on the rope, flailed, then hung firmly. Slowly she descended to the rocks below.

An hysterical Maude looked up at her rescuer and let go of the rope. Al pulled it up and put it around Mr. Marsh. He stood on the edge of the canyon, rolled his eyes heavenward, and eased down to his daughter. He did not look up again even to thank Al. Instead he grabbed Maude's hand and together they crossed the stream by way of the boulders. They climbed the far bank and disappeared among the firs.

Alligator coiled his rope, put it over his shoulder, and studied the ascent. Carefully he reached up and slipped his fingers into a crack. He pulled himself up until his toe found a fissure, then he reached for another handhold. The next one was far to his left. He tilted, went sideways, and found a wide ledge with his knee.

Spinner felt perspiration break out on her forehead as she watched him slowly pull himself onto the ledge. Below him the water roared. He disappeared under an overhang. In agony Spinner waited for him to reappear.

After what seemed an eternity his hand came over the ledge. Like a thing alive it sought a place to grip and hold. Spinner grabbed a rock crack and put out her foot. The hand reached, touched, the fingers clenched her boot, and Al scrambled over the ledge. He smiled weakly, stood up, and studied the canyon wall.

"We can get to the bottom on that crack." He pointed to a jagged break in the rock, and after tightening the hip belt on his pack, he sidled down the fissure. Spinner followed slowly. About halfway down Alligator paused before a boulder that jutted across his path. He curved his body slightly and sidestepped slowly around it, then leaped to a wide ledge. With a bold sweep of his arm he beckoned Spinner.

"I can't do that," she screamed frantically. "I can't do that."

Perspiration glistened on Alligator's forehead, his eyes softened. "Come on," he begged. "Please, Spinner, try it." She balked.

"Spinner"—his voice was low and confident— "please, do it. You can."

As if in a dream she stepped on the ledge and edged down to the boulder.

She curved her body, moved one centimeter, two, three; then out of the corner of her eye she saw the water far below.

Her belt struck a rock snag. She could not move. Sucking in her dancer's stomach, she leaned out. The weight of her pack pulled her backward. Her fingers slipped and she knew she must fall.

The water roared in the throat of rocks far below. She waited for the plunge. Spinner could not believe that life was over.

With great control she tightened her stomach muscles. She stopped falling backward, teetered, and gradually, as if in slow motion, she came toward the boulder. Her fingers clamped and she was safe.

Spinner looked at Alligator. His face was white, his teeth clenched. With movements so swift they were almost reflexes he slipped off his pack, pulled his knife from its sheath, and leaped to the boulder above her. He lay down on his belly, his face close to hers.

"I'm going to jettison your pack. Hold on to me." She grabbed his shirt. He reached down and slashed her hip belt. Then he cut one shoulder strap, grabbed it, severed the other, and clutched both straps. "Now hold me around the neck," he ordered. Spinner worked her fingers up his shirt, then around his neck. She clasped them behind his head. When she was secure, he let go of both straps simultaneously. The pack hesitated, then dropped away. Spinner stared into Alligator's gray eyes, read their fear . . . and . . . relief.

"I can make it now," she said and sidled around the boulder, crept onto the ledge, and fell into a trembling heap. Alligator flopped down beside her. After a long silence he handed her a candy bar.

The water rushed on, a butterfly winged past, and net-winged flies circled and buzzed. An hour passed. Relaxed and refreshed, Spinner looked down into the canyon for her pack. It was nowhere to be seen, not a scrap of it. Al leaned far out to see if he could locate it. The water boiled and roared. He shook his head and their eyes met.

"That was too close for comfort," he said.

The remainder of the route down the fissure was easy, for it was wide and firm. About ten meters from the bottom Spinner backed over a rock and put her feet on the stones at the stream's edge. She jumped from boulder to stone as she followed Alligator to a meadow where iris bloomed and the death camas thrust its un-opened spikes above sweet mosses.

Spinner flopped down in the cool grass. Al dumped his pack and went back upstream to hunt for hers. He returned with her frame and one sodden sock.

"That's all that's left," he said. "Tonight we camp with one tent and one sleeping bag, and eat yampa roots, berries, and fish."

Al fished while Spinner dug yampa roots and hunted bulbs. She built a small fire. When the coals were red she wrapped the fish in wet balsamroot leaves and buried it with the roots. In a short while the food was done. "It really needs ginger," she said, "but it's fabulous anyway."

After a drink of icy water they started on down the mountain. Alligator walked beside the stream; Spinner kept close to the hill. Presently they rounded a bend in the stream and came to a halt.

The creek slowed down, puddled, and formed a small alpine lake. It was reed-edged, spiked with arrowheads, and rimmed with white sego lilies. Frogs sang from its shallows and swifts swooped over its surface catching insects.

Al raced all the way around the lake and back to Spinner.

"This is the Continental Divide," he exclaimed. "That explains everything. Desperation Creek splits here. Half of it flows east to the Atlantic; half flows west to the Pacific. The cutthroats that laid the eggs at the foot of the waterfall must have come up the east side because. . . ." He paused.

"There have been no cutthroats in the Snake for ten years," Spinner finished.

"Yes," he said. "How did you know?"

Alligator pointed down the western slope toward the Snake.

"Somewhere down there," he said, "something goes

wrong. None of the little cutthroats get to the Snake or Gros Ventre or even Crystal Creek! Let's find out why." He started down at a fast trot.

The sun was behind the mountain when Alligator stopped to make night camp. He spread his sleeping bag for their bed and unrolled his tent for a blanket. Spinner lay down but she could not sleep. When she closed her eyes she was falling into chasms and rivers. Terrified, she concentrated on the stars and the sound of Alligator's soft breathing.

Suddenly he twitched, his body grew tense, and he reached out.

"Don't fall," he called in his sleep. "Spinner, hang on! Spinner don't fall. Don't leave me."

Spinner reared up on her elbows, pushed her long hair out of her eyes, and looked into her cousin's face. Furrows of distress grooved his forehead. He cared for her! He was not a cold alligator at all, but a loving person named Allen Shafter. She leaned closer to him.

The stars blinked, the wind rustled flowers, and the brook splashed on toward the sea. Spinner gently touched Al's head. She was there in his dream. She was a part of him. She rolled over on her back and smiled. Like the mayflies and midges, she had emerged in Al's world not as the dumb city mouse but as something transformed—a thing he cared for and loved.

She felt new and different.

With a cry he awoke, glanced around, and sat up.

"I had a nightmare," he said.

"Was it terrible?"

He looked at her with concern, then slowly gathered his thoughts. "No," he said, "you were falling. It was great! No more trouble." He lay back. "Umph."

Spinner pulled the tent around her chin and smiled.

"You'll never be a good fisherman," she said.

The tent rustled. "Why?"

"You tell the truth in your sleep." Al rolled to his elbows and glared down at her.

"What did I say?"

"That you care about me."

He umphed, yanked the tent, and turned his back to her. Al promptly went back to sleep, but Spinner lay awake thinking about the love of cousins.

You could be yourself with a cousin, she mused, nasty, nice, mad, happy, dumb, bright—all the things you needed to be to grow up. And nothing you did ever ruined the relationship.

A cousin was forever, close yet distant, loving yet honest, tolerant and intolerant. She grinned and fell securely asleep.

6

THE DIVIDE

A fire was leaping brightly under a bucket of simmering leaves when Spinner awoke. The air smelled of fir spice and smoke. The forest was clean, the air sharp, and Spinner was happy to the last bones of her toes. During the night she had emerged from her old skin of fears and doubts to become a person at ease with the rocks and forests.

Al poured her a cup of wild herbal tea, doused the fire, and removed the charred wood. When the ground looked as if they had never been there, he rigged his rod. A bag of candy was the only civilized food they had left.

Al fished as they ambled slowly down the mountain.

"I'm thinking about that second year of FISH's life," he said as he paused at a deep pool. "It would be great to know what made him grow so fast. Then we could make the eggs and hatchlings in Crystal Creek grow like crazy too. They could replace FISH in one year."

"If you eat the trash fish and throw back the trout," Spinner said, "the trout would grow fast."

"Yah, yah, yah," Al snapped, and reminded her she had said that a hundred times. She smiled. Yesterday she would have sulked at his peevishness but today she knew that their cousinship prevailed. He loved her no matter how dumb.

Alligator wound in his line. They went into the trees to find an easier route down the mountain than along the ragged stream side.

"Somewhere below us," said Al as he started off, "lies the clue to FISH's growth. We have to solve that."

Around noon the trees thinned and they approached the end of subalpine firs. Pines took over and Al, declaring they were in the foothills, began to trot.

"There's a meadow ahead," he called, "and maybe the answer to FISH."

Al stopped abruptly.

"Spinner!" His voice was hoarse. "Grizzly!"

Her heart crashed in her chest. She looked around, saw no tree small enough to climb, and got behind Al.

He pointed to a young lodgepole. "Get up it. We're downwind. The bear hasn't smelled us yet. When he does, he'll run off. These backcountry bears are terrified of people. But let's take precautions."

Spinner grabbed a limb, Al gave her a boost, and she climbed as high as she could. He clambered after her. As they reached the top, the slender tree bent and dipped, and Spinner and Al rode down toward the grizzly.

The bear did not run. Instead the massive sow rose to her hind feet. Her fur glistened and her body loomed like a forested mountain. She walked toward the tree like a man, her forepaws dangling.

Spinner and Al rode down toward the mammoth dishpan face. The huge nose sucked in their scents.

The tree dipped lower. Now the grizzly's head was level with Spinner's boot. The bear snarled and lifted a gigantic paw. The tree shivered, reached its lowest point, and slowly began to climb upward. It apogeed and started down again.

"*Rooooaar*," Al bellowed as they came down toward the snarling bear. The grizzly startled, and for a moment she glared into Spinner's eyes. Her paws twitched. Al roared again. Slowly, taking a thousand years, it seemed to Spinner, the huge animal lowered herself to all fours, turned and trotted away several meters. Then, with sudden madness, she sniffed, turned, and rushed the tree. Bellowing wildly, she struck the trunk with her huge paw. The overweighted tree cracked. With a blast, it splintered in half. Twigs flew and Spinner grabbed Al, wrenched him from his grip, and crashed to the ground with him. She fell on her shoulder and rolled to her knees. Screaming wildly, she looked for the grizzly. The bear was gone.

Al cried out. His voice was filled with pain. She ran to him and with relief saw he was not ripped by the bear, but was holding his leg.

She dropped to her knees beside him.

"It's busted. I heard it snap," Al said under his breath. Perspiration poured down his temples and Spinner's heart raced. What would become of them? They could not move any farther. They would die. She stifled a scream and huddled close to him.

"Can't understand why that sow charged," Al said, sensing her fears. "Can't understand. This is the back-country. Here bears are afraid of men. Here. . . ." His face grew pale and he closed his eyes. "I'll be all right in a minute," he said.

Spinner unsnapped his belt and eased the pack from his shoulders. She loosened his boots and opened his shirt. Finally she unrolled his sleeping bag, and now, in control, knew what she must do . . . go through the forest alone.

"I'll stuff the bag under you for warmth," she said, "and go for help." She unzipped the sleeping bag, eased it under Al, and pulled the top half over him.

"There's some aspirin in my side pocket," he said. "I'll take some. Now listen. Follow the stream. You'll hit Crystal Creek eventually. I'm sure of that. FISH was tagged in Desperation Creek and he reached the Snake. You will too. When you find Crystal Creek, follow it to the Red Rock Ranch. Gunner lives there." Al rolled his head from side to side. "Darn it," he said, "Darn umph."

"The bear," Spinner queried. "What should I do about the bear? She'll come back and kill you."

He told her to build a fire near his head, gather a pile of dry wood, and give him his mess kit and spoon to bang. Spinner got to her feet, and without even a whimper, picked up armloads of limbs and fallen logs. She broke them with her knees and feet and piled them beside Al.

 *7*

THE STUMPS

The sun had started down the western sky when Spinner shoved a big log into the flames. She put the last of the candy beside Al's hand, stood up, and looked down the mountainside.

"I'm off," she whispered.

She ran for twenty meters before the din of crackles and snaps became too terrifying to endure. Grizzlies were everywhere. She hugged a tree and stared around, unable to go on.

A branch snapped behind her and she fled. Halfway back to Al she became confused.

"Al!" There was no answer. A red squirrel clattered

its teeth, and she turned completely around and ran the other way. She stumbled, fell, and saw the flame of fire behind a knoll. As she scrambled to Al she saw the pain in his eyes. She could not tell him she had failed.

"Al," she said, thinking fast to explain why she had returned. "I'm going to take your notebook and compass. I'll make a map. So we can find you quickly. It may be dark when I get back."

Al could only grit his teeth and nod. She took out his notebook. Then she took off her shirt, cut it into strips with her embroidery scissors, and tied a piece around the tree at Al's head.

"That will shine even in the dark." She wrote down the time and put "North" at the top of the page and near it an "X" for Al.

"I mark down a landmark where I am, take a reading on another landmark, and pace it off. Right?" He nodded. She picked a distant tree and pointed the direction-of-travel arrow at it. Carefully she twisted the compass housing until the magnetic needle pointed to N. Placing the compass north and south on the paper, she drew a line from "X."

"Now I count my steps to that tree and take another reading, don't I?"

"You're a good woodsperson," Al said. Inspired by his compliment, she paced off the tree, tied a band on it, and went on.

In a few minutes she came to an alpine meadow that was pink with flowers and yellow with bees. On her map she drew the forest edge and a rock where she had emerged. Then she wrote, "2013 steps to Al."

Spinner strode off through the meadow, then stopped. Beneath the tall fireweeds and grasses stood thousands of tree stumps. The whole mountainside had been cleared of trees. She looked around. Below ran West Desperation Creek and near the creek sat the sun-blackened buildings of a lumber camp. The doors banged in the wind.

Spinner walked toward the camp, hoping to find someone who could help Al. Halfway she stopped. Something rustled. A bear? Her mouth went dry with fear and she quickened her stride.

A raven called as it sailed down from the mountain peaks and dropped out of sight. Spinner dashed to the top of a knoll and looked down on the camp garbage dump. The raven was throwing fresh orange peels over its shoulder. People must be using the camp. She burst into a run to find them, then stopped abruptly. A small grizzly bear lifted its head and snorted.

Spinner backed up slowly. Al had said bears that feed

at dumps had no fear of man and therefore were terribly dangerous. Now she knew why the big sow had attacked. She was not a backcountry bear at all, but a logging-camp bear spoiled by man.

The young bear snarled and ran a few steps away. Spinner ducked into the tall weeds and raced down the mountainside to the edge of the creek. She put fifty meters between herself and the bear, and did not stop until she reached the bridge where the road crossed Desperation Creek. Here she scooped up a drink. The water was warm compared to the icy pools where the trout dwelled. She realized why. The trees were gone and the hot sun heated the water.

"That's why the little cutthroats can't get to the Snake," she reasoned aloud. "The water's too hot. Here is where they die. Here's the block."

Spinner did not linger. As she came abreast of the camp she called, but the buildings were deserted. Why the fresh garbage at the dump, then? She had no time to wonder, but took a compass reading, drew on her map, and followed the logging road down the edge of West Desperation Creek. She ran, walked, then ran again.

The water of the creek was muddy. The soil had washed off the treeless slope and settled on stream rocks. Pools were weed-filled and murky. No cutthroat from the Snake could return to its breeding ground through this water. Here was the killer of trout.

Spinner made swift progress down the logging road. A small band of elk watched her run. She called to them. They sprinted around the stumps and vanished in the brush. The road ended and Spinner climbed down a small waterfall into a forest of aspen. There by the stream was a well-trodden trail. She recognized it— the trail to their second camp. Breaking into a sprint, she dashed to the junction of West Desperation and Crystal creeks. Beyond lay the grove in which they had camped. With a cry of joy she rushed out on the Indian trail.

The sun was almost down to the tops of the mountains when Spinner climbed the hill that looked down on the Red Rock Ranch. In leaps she rushed down it, crossed the field, and ran up the road to the house. A coyote crossed her path. "Ha!" she cried to it. "I'm not afraid of you now. Ha!"

The door of the house was open. Spinner stepped inside and called into an empty kitchen. Footsteps sounded in a distant room, a door opened, and Gunner appeared. She blurted out her story.

Gunner acted quickly. He phoned the hospital for an ambulance, called the barn, and told a ranch hand to bring the stretcher from the first-aid room.

Spinner did not think to call Aunt Becky until she was in the jeep with Gunner and the cowboy, Jake. Perhaps it was just as well. Al would be safe when she learned of the accident.

Gunner parked near the Crystal Creek campsite and picked up the stretcher. Jake took out a rifle. "Bear country," he said to Spinner. She nodded knowingly and read her map.

"We take this trail to Desperation Creek," she said, leading off.

"Bears," she addressed the mountain. "Jake has a gun. Lie quiet like a winter snake, like an old volcano, like a dragon, like a sleeping lion. Lie quiet, bears. Don't get shot." Her thoughts surprised her. She was no longer fear-ridden. In the course of a few days she had become at ease with the mountains.

Fortunately the sun was still shining in the high country when they arrived in the clear-cut zone. The light helped Spinner lead the rescue party quickly up the slope. Halfway to the rock at the edge of the forest, Gunner stopped and looked at the mountainside.

"This is all clear-cut," he said. "Lumber companies are not allowed to do this to Forest Service land! They must cut selectively; take the big trees and leave the young ones." He leaned down and touched the soil.

"Government orders this . . . get fifty million saw-board meters of lumber a year. . . . It's suicide. No wonder my creek and irrigation ditch run lower each year. There are no trees up here to hold the moisture and make the rain."

His eyes narrowed. "Didn't even know about this. They must have hauled the trees out on the other side of the mountain. Terrible. Terrible. Changes the whole mountain. And me." He started up the slope. "Senator Harvey Bilbo, I have news for you." He clenched his fist and shook his head. "The lumber companies did not even replant."

At the rock, Spinner asked Gunner to switch on his light. She set her compass on N and pointed her arm at 220 degrees.

"That way is Al," she said. "One, two. . . ." She began counting her steps. Gunner and Jake fell in behind and after 2013 steps she stopped. The sun had set, the forest was dark. An owl hooted. A branch snapped.

"Al!" she called. A nighthawk whistled to his mate. She grabbed Gunner's hand. "He should be here, right here." Her voice was thick, for her tongue was swollen from thirst and exhaustion. "The bear . . . do you think she killed Al and dragged him off?"

"Naw," Gunner said calmly. "He's right near here somewhere. He's okay. He knows what to do. Look!"

He pointed to the red embers of a fire not three meters away.

Spinner dropped on her knees and crept to Al's side.

"Al," she said softly. "I'm here." He looked up at her.

"Umph," he said and passed out.

8

THE WEB

The yellow light of dawn brightened Teton Pass and illuminated the chimney tops in the town of Jackson. Spinner was up. She was standing on a squeaky board in the wooden walk that encircled the town square. This would be the seventh time she counted the boards as she rounded the park waiting for Uncle Augustus and Aunt Becky to come out of the hospital. She knew every store and restaurant, every hitching post and horseshoe.

Anxiously she waited, recalling the events of the night.

Gunner and Jake had carried Alligator off the mountain at two o'clock in the morning. The ambulance was waiting at Gunner's door. Spinner had called Aunt Becky and Uncle Augustus and they met at the hospital around three. At four Aunt Becky had sent her to the hotel to sleep. At five she had dressed and come to the square. Now it was six. She was cold and concerned.

Spinner started around the square once more. She thought about Al as she stepped on each board. Would he still be in pain? Would he be upset to be on crutches? Would he remember the cliff and his nightmare? Would he . . . ?

The door of the little hospital opened and three figures emerged. Spinner darted across the square and rounded the corner. There limped Al, his shoulders slumped, his head bowed.

"Al?" she called softly. He turned and his sunken eyes sparked to life.

"Spinner!" He smiled. His eyes were warm and friendly. "We've got to get down to Ditch Creek right away. I've figured out the mystery of FISH."

Spinner threw her arms around Aunt Becky and buried her head on her breast. Strong hands patted her gently.

"He's slowed down for about a month," Aunt Becky said. But he can peel potatoes and darn socks."

The terrible ordeal came to an end.

Uncle Augustus opened the car door, Al got in and Spinner slipped in beside him.

"It did happen, didn't it?" she said, touching his cast. "I wasn't really sure."

"I still don't understand," he said, "why that back-country bear attacked. Umph."

"She wasn't in the wilderness," Spinner said, and described the lumber camp, the mountainside, and the dump. Al rubbed his chin, the car accelerated, and they sped out of Jackson into the open valley.

"I'm sorry, Al," Spinner said. "I shouldn't have grabbed you. You fell crooked. I'm not a very good woodsperson."

"That's not what I heard, Country Mouse. I hear the Geological Survey is looking for you. Want you to make maps. I got us lost, but you found us."

Spinner beamed and pushed back her hair. She was the midge in the waterfall, the nymph in the pool that had changed into something new.

The car passed the Elk Refuge, her head buzzed, and a thought clanged out. She had been led by a fish up a creek, into a waterfall, over a mountain, and now into human affairs.

"I'm going to call Senator Bilbo too," she said to Al,

"and tell him about the last cutthroats. Maybe he'll do something about them." He did not hear her. He was fast asleep.

The next morning Al was at the hand-hewn table in front of the window of the Tetons when Spinner came out of her bedroom. It was late and he had finished a sketch of a bear on his cast. It had huge teeth and GRRRR written in a balloon from its mouth.

"I called the Forest Service," he said after she admired his artwork. "That mountainside was clear-cut seven years ago."

Spinner pulled her hair under her chin and around her neck.

"That means," he said, "FISH was in the cutover area his second year, the year after the stream life died. And that's odd. What did he eat?" He scratched his head. "Maybe if we go back to Ditch Creek and start all over again, we'll see the answer. We'll just sit there until all nature tells us what's wrong."

Al was out the door and skillfully wheeling over the stones before Spinner could ask how he would get there. His crutches whirled like windmill blades and she ran to keep up with him.

"You're a wizard," she said.

"This is my second broken leg. Last time I did it

skiing." He slowed down at the bench and eased him-self to the bottom. They moved more leisurely through the cottonwood grove.

At the end of the fisherman's trail Al sat down on the bank and folded his arms on his chest. Spinner collapsed beside him.

"When was the last time you fished this hole?" she asked. Al could not remember.

"Anyone who knows anything about fishing," he said, "never fishes at the end of a trail like this. All fished out."

The sun stood white and hot above them and Spinner rolled into the shade of a cottonwood. Al stretched out. A magpie alighted on a branch and Spinner wondered aloud what people looked like to a bird.

"Probably like an eye," Al said. "Birds see only part of a whole creature, the most characteristic part: the short neck of a hawk, the long neck of a goose; maybe your flowing hair."

Spinner lifted her hair, let it fall, and the bird flew toward her. She ducked and looked down on Al's bucket. The water she had gathered from the Snake River was still in it. But now it was yellow-green.

"Pea soup for lunch?" she asked and thrust his can toward him. "Look, I found it."

Al stared into a mass of algae. The plants had been

able to reproduce in the still water that had been changed from the splashing, roaring rills of the Snake into a warm pool by the can.

"The bloom!" Al rocked up to a one-footed stand. "Remember the bloom of the mayflies and midges? Well, this is sort of like that, only it's plants, not animals. When the forest was felled the creek warmed up and killed everything that loved swift, icy water. But nature abhors vacuums. To fill the gap, billions of algae grew. Then billions of diatoms arose to absorb the algae and billions of caddis larvae hatched to eat them. Then FISH thrived on the bloom. He ate and ate and . . ."

". . . ate and ate," said Spinner.

"And," Al went on, "came down to the Snake. But he could never get back to spawn again and his line died out."

"So," said Spinner, "there have not been any cutthroats in this part of the Snake River for ten years."

"And," Al went on, "no one fished his hole, so he survived." He grabbed his crutches. "The case is closed." Al turned and swung up the trail. Spinner walked beside him.

"You've solved it, Al," she said, "except for one thing. People do fish that hole. Dad did. Said he caught a snag and lost his hook." Al shrugged. Spinner went on. "He lost his hook but not on a snag. He lost it to FISH." Al glared at her.

"Are you trying to say your dad hooked FISH and didn't catch him?" His voice was incredulous. "An expert fisherman like him?"

"Yes, I am. I am also trying to say FISH broke Dad's line but not mine. How come? How come I caught him?"

"Cause you're a city mouse and FISH was being nice to you."

Spinner umphed, held Al's crutches, and watched him clamber up the steep river bench on all threes. They walked through the sage in silence, for Spinner was thinking of home. Tomorrow she must return to the city.

The next morning as she was packing, Al brought her a hand-drawn poster.

EAT TRASH FISH. THROW BACK THE TROUT, it read. He held it at arm's length.

"Let's write our wild recipe on it," she shouted, clapping her hands. "And draw balsamroot leaves, yampa, and chicory so everyone can find them."

Al grinned, put the poster on the table, and they both went to work.

When it was done Al held it up enthusiastically. "I'm

going to print hundreds on the school press," he said. "And hang them at every fishing hole. Will you help?"

She said she had to pack, but in reality FISH, and now the hole she had pulled him from, intrigued her. The mystery was not yet solved.

When the house was quiet Spinner put on her bathing suit, pulled her blue jeans over it, took a rope and goggles from the pump house, and hurried down the fisherman's trail to the Snake.

At the riverbank she took off her outer clothes and sat down. Grasshoppers flicked around her, crickets sang, birds chirped. The great mountains were paper-like and beautiful in the high noon light. She would not see them after tomorrow, those great shoulders that harbored waterfalls and flowers, wild fish and strange blooms of beasts and plants.

A flower trembled and her grandfather appeared, fly rod in hand.

"One more cast," he said, "before I have to go home to your grandmother. Maybe I can win that medal from you." He paused on the now-famous gravel bar.

"No use fishing here," she said. "It's all fished out." He winked at her and his spirited old legs carried him up the river trail to a better spot.

Spinner watched the river surface peak into tongues, swirl into shore, and slow down to create a quiet backwater just beyond Ditch Creek. She got up, crossed the creek, and walked along the bank. The sun was straight overhead and she could see to the bottom of FISH's hole. Something was down there. Ha, she thought so!

After a few fumbling efforts she tied the rope firmly to a tree and then around herself. The Snake had killed too many people for her to risk being pulled into its terrible current. Spinner put on her goggles and waded out to the bar. She stepped into the cold water, held her nose, and went under. The surface swirled above her. She was in FISH's domain, a pool of lights and sounds. Green and purple currents moved dancer-like to the clunks and clicks of stones. She peered around.

A dark object lay at the downstream edge of the hole. Spinner recognized the shape. It had been deeply imprinted on her mind while learning to fish with her dad. It was the hull of an old ferry. Small fish schooled around it and weeds twisted off its water-logged boards. Behind the hull, the forceful water had carved a deep hole—FISH's home. Sand glistened on the bottom and stones edged the far side. She looked up. Grasshopper legs poked into the water.

"Oh, FISH, that's it!" she thought. "Big food for a big FISH, not on the bottom where Al and I had looked, but up on the surface." She popped into the air, took a deep breath, and glanced around.

"The whole mountain range made FISH," she said, "and something else." She took a breath and went under again. Beyond the ferry hull the current jetted off into the channel. Spinner grabbed the hull, kicked her feet, and looked closely at the boards. One was encased in silver webs.

She surfaced, gasped for air, and pushing her back-flowing mat of hair, she went under once more.

"Webs," she said to herself. "Silver spindles. Of course!" Spinner kicked down to the hull, touched the silver, and let out a hundred laughter-bubbles. They rushed to the surface ahead of her.

"Zig!" she said to the Tetons, "I've solved it!"

Hauling on the line, she pulled herself to the bank, unhitched the rope, and dressed. She ran, putting all the pieces together as she raced.

FISH had hatched in Desperation Creek below the glacial falls. He had moved to the lumber camp, fed on the bloom of life, grown, and gone on to the Snake. That she and Al knew. Now she could tell the rest of the story. In the deep pool where Ditch Creek meets the Snake, FISH had grown larger on the constant supply of summer grasshoppers knocked into the river by the wind and people like her.

But, *most* important, FISH had learned, and thereby saved himself.

"A snag," her dad had said when FISH had struck his line. Not so. Every time FISH had been caught he had taken the line, dashed around the hull two or three times, and snapped it off. He had done this to all the experts. Meters and meters of fishing line were wound around the old ferry by FISH.

So why did I catch him?

She slowed down to a walk and scratched her head. FISH should certainly have collected her line. She did not even know how to fish.

A thought germinated in the tumble of her mind. It sang, rooted, and grew; leafed, blossomed. That was it! She didn't know how to fish! Spinner turned around and ran full speed all the way back to the Snake, unrolled the rope, measured the distance from the hull to the gravel bar, and sped home.

9

THE NYMPH

In her bedroom, Spinner opened her suitcase, took out her fishing reel, and carried it to the porch. Carefully she stretched her line to measure it against the length of the rope. "Ha!" she said and did a backward sommersault.

Half an hour later Aunt Becky came home.

"Aunt Becky," Spinner cried, "I know why no one but me caught FISH." Aunt Becky's eyes brightened and she leaned toward her wisely.

"Because he liked you."

"No! Because I'm a city mouse." Spinner switched her hair from side to side like willow limbs. "Dad hooked FISH. FISH wrapped his line around that ferry hull at the bottom of his hole and—snapped off his hook. 'Snag,' Dad said. So did thousands of other fishermen who lost their hooks."

"Then, I came along. FISH grabbed my fly, but never got to the boat hull. You know why? Dad cut my line short. He didn't think I could handle a regular line like the experts. And"—her eyes sparkled with humor, fun, foolishness, and appreciation—"so, I caught FISH."

Aunt Becky clapped her hands.

"Oh, Spinner, I love it!" Her eyes crinkled and she shook her head. "FISH fooled all the super fishers all of the time, but none of the lowly ones ever." She opened the freezer, took out a frozen huckleberry pie, and put it in the oven.

"Let's celebrate," she said as Grandfather came in the door, his brow furrowed from another futile fishing expedition. Aunt Becky told him the story of FISH. He grinned so broadly he got a cramp in his jaw and declared he needed a nip of brandy.

Spinner looked out the window. "I wish Al would get back. I want to tell Al."

"Don't do that," Aunt Becky declared. "You just can't trust a fisherman. After all, those little fish are growing up in Crystal Creek right now. Maybe next year they'll be down to the ferry hull; Al will cut his line short like yours, and . . ."—Aunt Becky's eyes rolled, her lips pressed thoughtfully together—". . . and. . . ." Spinner clutched her hair at her temples and ran her fingers all the way down the long black strands to her waist.

"Aunt Becky," she said, "is that why Al worked so hard to solve the mystery?" Her voice faded. "It is." She looked at her aunt. "Yes, it is." The wonder she felt for Al's scientific genius vanished. He was just a Shafter. He wanted that medal.

Spinner fondled her hair and sighed. Slowly she twisted the cascade of black silk into one lock, walked to the bathroom mirror, and pondered.

A car pulled into the driveway, and Aunt Becky hurried to the porch to see who had arrived. Spinner heard a familiar voice through the open bathroom window.

"Here's your cutthroat. Mounted on walnut. Nice." Spinner darted from the bathroom to the living room and emerged on the porch as Aunt Becky took the mount from Maude Marsh. FISH was stiff and unreal. His back was a gaudy blue, his mouth was open hideously. Spinner shuddered and Aunt Becky sighed.

Maude was staring at Spinner.

"How are you?" Spinner asked.

"Oh . . ." Maude said, "you live here?"

"I'm Allen Shafter's cousin," she explained. "He's

the track star whose badge you kicked and who saved your life."

"Oh, yes, him," she blurted. "We could've gotten off the cliff, of course. Not so soon, but we could've." Spinner shifted her weight from one foot to both feet.

"What did you do with those cutthroats you netted?" she asked.

Maude looked surprised, backed away a few steps, and bit a nail with a loud crunch. She did not answer.

"Al would like to know." The mention of his name changed Maude's attitude.

"Oh, sure. I'll tell Al. That's why we were stuck. We were at the top of the canyon when I stumbled and knocked the bucket out of Dad's hand. It fell into the water and we tried to go after it. It's still there." She bit off another nail. ". . . jammed in the water between rocks. Didn't you see it?"

Maude thought the fish were probably alive. "They are in rushing water," she said.

"Maude Marsh," Spinner said. "You and I are going back up that mountain and get those fish." The girl stepped toward her father's car as if he would protect her from Spinner.

"I'll tell the sheriff," Spinner threatened. "You can't take little cutthroats. Besides, Al broke his leg when you left. He sure would like those fish to go free in Crystal Creek."

"Oh," Maude gasped, "I'm sorry. Really I am." She leaned against the car, and her father, sensing that something was wrong, clambered out and stood by her side. Then he recognized Spinner. He shoved his hands in his pockets and cleared his throat.

"Sorry we had to leave you kids so fast," he said, "but my wife was sick."

"Come on, Pa," Maude snapped. "You don't have to be a fisherman all the time." She grabbed on to his arm. "Please take Spinner and me to the Red Rock Ranch. We're going to get those cutthroats and set them free." Her father's face darkened.

"You can't do that. It's dangerous up there." He placed his two feet in a wide stance and folded his arms on his chest.

"Al busted his leg after saving us," Maude said. Mr. Marsh's face softened like butter in the sun. He looked from Maude to Spinner, then touched Aunt Becky's arm warmly.

"I'm sorry," he said, "I really am." He turned to Spinner.

"I'll drive you."

Aunt Becky decided to go along to fend off the bears

with a kettle, a spoon, and a gun. "Even bears who have lost their fear of man are afraid of me," she said. "I fill them with the fear of the busybody."

Spinner dashed to the pump house for Al's pack. A mirror above a washbasin caught her eye. She peered into it, twisted her hair on top of her head, and stared a long moment. She *was* a changeling, a midge in the waterfall, a nymph in the mayfly pool. "I will be a new thing too," she said.

Twenty minutes later she came out of the pump house in her hiking jacket and hat. She jumped in the car beside Maude.

"Tucked up your hair," the girl observed. "Good idea. It's hot up there in the sun." She pushed hers under her hat.

The car rolled out of the ranch and down the dusty road toward the land of the last cutthroats.

Late in the afternoon Spinner found the bucket lodged in the rocks. She leaned down, wrenched it from its mooring, and opened the mesh lid. The fish were still alive.

"Seven," she said, and noted that BUGS swam in safety below the others.

"Hello, FISH," she said, changing his name. "I'll see you someday at Ditch Creek and the Snake."

Spinner and Maude sat down peaceably to wait for

Aunt Becky to come down from the woods where she had gone to look for berries. In mere moments she appeared on the elks' trail. She was swinging her pans.

"That old sow bear is up there in the firs." Her face softened. "She's napping. Pretty thing she is, and the last of the great wild Americans, *Ursus arctos horribilis,* the grizzly."

Spinner remembered the huge face, the growls and snarls that terrified her only yesterday. She shivered and ran to Aunt Becky.

A shot rang out.

Spinner clutched Aunt Becky, her eyes wide with apprehension. Another shot sounded. Gunsmoke drifted out of the forest and a ranger appeared. He startled when he saw the women.

"Get out of here," he commanded. "This is grizzly country. I just shot a vicious sow." He was hard and nervous. "She attacked some kids here yesterday."

Spinner glanced at the dark trees, the speckles of sunlight, and the alpine meadow where the grizzly's yampa grew. Beyond lay the fallen trees, the silt-filled streams, and the camp garbage pit.

"The bear was feeding off the backpacker's dump at the abandoned lumber camp," the ranger went on. "Dangerous bear. Neither wild nor tame, but fearless . . . and that's bad."

"When the bears go," Aunt Becky said with controlled anger, "the mountains will fall." It was not her fault that she could not adjust to raped forests. Aunt Becky's shoulders slumped and Spinner took her arm. A change was upon Aunt Becky's world.

"How," thought Spinner hopelessly, "can I replace a bear for Aunt Becky?"

She picked up the bucket of fish and led her aunt down through the forest. Spinner stumbled not so much from fatigue but from a sense of bewilderment. "How can I glue the mountain back together again? The waterfall creatures would know. They would invent some kind of cement."

An hour later Spinner and Aunt Becky lowered FISH and team into the green pool where West Desperation joins Crystal Creek. The young cutthroats felt the fresh jet of water rush into the bucket, turned their heads into it, and swam out into the headstream. They drifted toward the bottom as they tasted their new environment through their gills and skin, then FISH moved out ahead. The others fell in behind him and fanned in diamond-shaped formation. Spinner shook the bush branches. Several insects fell into the water and FISH swirled up and snatched one.

"Let Al win the medal back," she whispered, then picked up the bucket and walked back to the car.

Mr. Marsh dropped her and Aunt Becky at home just as the planet Venus touched the tip of Buck Mountain.

"Time for the men to come home from the river," Aunt Becky observed as she hurried into the house and lit the old stove. Spinner met Uncle Auggie. He had not gone fishing. She sat down beside him. "I put in a call to Senator Bilbo," he said, "and am waiting for his return call." The phone rang. Uncle Auggie picked it up.

"Harvey," he began. Spinner listened to every word as she watched the window for Al.

Presently the Shafter flashlights twinkled far out in the sage. She opened the door and ran toward them as Al's fishing song piped through the twilight.

The sun had set and the cold wind from the mountains was blowing across the sage. Spinner was skipping when she found Al.

"What's with you?" he asked. "Why are you so happy?"

"Come find out!" She danced into the house, where her dad and grandfather were drinking coffee. Uncle Auggie was still on the telephone.

"Well, little champ," her father said as she sat down beside him. "Now you can go back to perfumes, leotards, and dance."

"I don't think I will," Spinner said. "Aunt Becky invited me to stay until school starts."

"Oh, no," he said. "You've had enough adventures for a lifetime."

Spinner took off her hat. A fuzzy black cap set off her dark eyes and full mouth. The long hair was gone. Snippets and twists replaced it. Al gulped. Aunt Becky whistled softly. Her dad grabbed his head and covered his eyes.

Spinner touched his arm.

"Uncle Auggie called Senator Bilbo," she said. "He is giving us ten thousand little trees to reforest the mountain of the cutthroats and return the rain to Gunner."

Her father lifted his head, saw her fuzzy head, and covered his eyes again.

"I want to do that," she said. "I hooked a fish and caught a mountain."

"My little girl," her father said, ignoring her, "where are you?"

"Right here." She shook his arm. "I'm me." She threw her arms around his neck.

Slowly he lifted his head. He ran his fingers through her short, clipped hair and stared hard. Gradually his eyes lost their bewilderment and his face brightened.

"You'd *better* stay," he said. "You *are* a fishing Shafter."

Al swung across the floor on his crutches and opened the refrigerator. He took out a watermelon, cut it in chunks and gave one piece to Spinner. She took a big bite. Al took a bite. Their eyes met and Spinner began to chuckle. She selected out seeds and stored them in her cheeks.

Her chuckles were infectious. Granddad smiled, Uncle Auggie grinned, and her dad's face was amused. Then Aunt Becky took a big bite of melon and winked at Spinner.

The good spirits broke into chortle, the chortle sparked over into laughter, and the laughter became celebration. A change was upon the land.

JEAN CRAIGHEAD GEORGE grew up in Washington, D.C., and was graduated from Penn State University. Among the many books she has written for young people are *My Side of the Mountain,* an ALA Notable Book and runner-up for the Newbery Medal, *Who Really Killed Cock Robin?, All Upon a Stone* (Crowell) and *All Upon a Sidewalk,* and *Julie of the Wolves* (Harper), winner of the 1973 Newbery Medal.

The real FISH in *Hook a Fish, Catch a Mountain* was caught by the author's son Luke. The setting for the story is Moose, Wyoming, where Ms. George's brothers live and where she and her family have spent many vacations.